IT WATCHED ME

ALEX BROWN

Copyright © 2021 Alex Brown
All Rights Reserved
Published in the United States
Open Kimono Publishing, LLC
ISBN Print 978-1-7377362-0-2
EBook 978-1-7377362-1-9
New Edition 978-1-961763-00-5

Library of Congress Cataloging-in-Publication Data
Names: Brown, Alex, author.
Title: It Watched Me / Alex Brown
Description: First Edition. | Colorado: Open Kimono Publishing, LLC
Identifiers: 978-1-7377362-0-2 (print) | 978-1-7377362-1-9 (ebook) | ISBN 978-1-7377362-2-6 (hardback)
Subjects: Alternate History Science Fiction / Alternate History / Horror Suspense
Classification:
LC record available at https://lccn.loc.gov
LC ebook record available at https://lccn.loc.gov
https://openkmedia.com/

ISBN 978-1-7377362-0-2

PRELUDE

I've never been a very superstitious person. I attribute that in large part to my twenty-seven years of walking around on this planet; I definitely haven't seen it all but I've seen enough. I graduated college with a four year degree back in twenty sixteen- in the five years since then I feel like I've made decent use of my time. As much as anyone could really I guess. I make my living selling used cars at 'Denver's Dealing Dave's Used Cars' off of 38th Street and Pecos downtown. I started working there in college, even though I graduated with my degree in Business Administration, I just could never get hired anywhere. It's probably because of my self assured demeanor- which to most people probably comes off as cocky instead of just an exudence of confidence. It's definitely not an ideal situation for me, especially because of the thirty-eight thousand dollars of student debt that I'm still lugging around on my back but this gig is the only way that I can afford paying that four-hundred and fifty dollars a month bill. Add in my eighteen hundred dollar rent, two hundred and sixty-five dollar car payment along with insurance, phone bill, gas, groceries... it all just keeps adding up. At the end of the month, I'm spending more than I'm making that's for sure but there's no other way really. I apply to all kinds of jobs but seemingly no one will hire me. It's almost as if I'm living in purgatory- my life is increasingly monotonous. A sobering fact that my wife Alondra constantly likes to remind me of. It's hard making a living on a used car salesman and a secretary's salary- like I said, we barely scrape by and that's even if I have a great month and sell five cars. Typically, I'll sell about three cars a month, give or take a one or two. It's mostly the trucks that people are snatching up the most in Colorado which is good for me since they're one of the most expensive. Being commission based, it's really a no brainer, but I don't ever talk people into buying something that they can't afford or don't really want. I'm not some greased up sleaze-ball pushing out as many lemons as I can to rake in the green. I care about what people want, I always listen to them before I show them our inventory. I'm not pushy but I'm definitely not lackadaisical either- I need to make money too. I dream about being able to have enough cash to pay off Alondra and I's student loans, cars, credit cards and be able to just uproot. We want to move to Seattle Washington to live on a modest houseboat- the way that the calm waves crack as they crest over the shore and refract back to the boat... the way that the dreary grey sky is usually gently trickling down a steady sheet of drizzling rain. The way the air smells- slightly damp with that tingy earthly gleam of dirt sun kissed by the adjoining Pacific Ocean... it's perfect. It's where we want to end up, it's where we hope to be but at this point, hope is all we have. It's a distant dream from our ever presently boring reality. Today is just like every other Monday. I woke up at seven in the morning, shaved, showered in water that was entirely too cold- our apartment maintenance sucks, and drove my old Jeep Wrangler to the car lot. I've been at work now for a couple hours without even one customer but that's pretty typical- Mondays are always pretty slow especially during the beginning of the month. I guess that's just part of the game, everything has its ebb and flow I suppose. I just sit at an oddly misplaced sales desk in the middle of the expansive dusty showroom. On both sides of me are some of our newer, more expensive cars that we have to offer. The one to my left is a blue hatchback with squeaky clean black tires that reflects the light especially during sundown- which I unfortunately get to experience pretty often. The car to my right is an emboldened blazing red Camaro with a slick retractable roof that is infatuating to the eyes of prospective customers- especially the ones that can't afford it. I am also included in that group, but that damned Camaro has been here over seven months and it's red reflection seems to constantly dim the light of everything around it, especially all my paperwork. The car's red gleam makes every contract or finance document I sign off burn into my eyes for minutes because of the stark white and red contrast. I hate it. Almost as much as I hate our sales manager Bob, now that guy is the definition of a sleazy car salesman! He's always draped in a blatantly cheap suit spritzed up with plastic cuff links painted to glimmer like gold seemingly hanging on for dear life to his frayed sleeves. As if his outlandish look was just an appetizer, he finishes it off with a stained red handkerchief dangling from his tired right coat pocket for the main dish, and for dessert the meal comes to a crescendo about two inches above his sweaty brow- he sports a thin palate of dyed black hair that's combed over from left to right in a grossly failed attempt to hide his obvious male pattern baldness. That damned patch of hair must be at least eight inches long- I wonder with a macabre sense of intrigue exactly what this half head mane must look like when he gets out of the shower. It's got to be hanging down to his left shoulder at least. I can almost hear the thin plop echo in a small unkempt bathroom as he scoops up the dark wet strands hemorrhaging a dark dye substance with his hand, adorned with cheap gaudy rings - and in one failed swoop, swipes it all to his head. The plop would sound like dropping a boiled cheese ravioli on a cold hard tiled floor, that I'm sure about. I hate this guy because he gives us all a bad name- after force selling a car down someone's throat he will come back in and gloat about it to the rest of us as if it was some heroic war story worthy of being a parable told down from one generation to the next. He also will lie straight to people's faces about a car's accident history, features, and anything he can get away with really. I've even seen him forge finance documents before, the guy is a crook, he will do anything to make a buck. I wish that I could do or say something at least, but everyone knows. No one does anything because the guy makes the business money, and money is seemingly all anyone cares about.

After eating an uneventful lunch consisting of a turkey sandwich dressed up with yellow mustard, Swiss cheese, and lettuce hastily pushed between two stale pieces of white bread, I was ready to go home for the day. Even so- I smacked my lips together in an odd contentment that the stale bread of my sandwich added a satisfying crunch to the whole ordeal that was almost as disgusting as needed. I told myself that this was new "crunchy whole wheat" so that I felt better about it. While pondering the logistics of how that bread was not yet green in hue from mold, my thoughts were interrupted by a ding from the front door! A man in his late forties dressed in khaki Dockers with a teal polo shirt proceeded to walk into the showroom. Instantaneously, I peeled myself from my chair and sprung to my feet as I said,

"Good Afternoon Sir! I'm Walker Henderson, it's good to meet you!"

Now beginning to saunter in my direction the man murmured,

"Walker, good to meet you…" as his eyes darted from left to right and then fixed themselves on the red Camaro.

"She's a beauty isn't she? She's a one owner, only 56,000 miles on her. You like it?"

The man said, "Damn- sure is beautiful. How much for it?"

I said, "Well, Mr....?" with just enough of a pause in my voice to indicate to him to tell me his name.

"Ted, Ted Robinson."

"Well Mr. Robinson, the sticker price is forty five- but we can look at your credit and I can find some incentives..."

Ted quickly cut me off mid spiel by interjecting, "Whoa there Walker, that's too rich for my blood. Let's pump the brakes kid."

I let out a friendly chuckle as I said,

"Me too, don't worry. So Mr. Robinson, what kind of car are you looking for today?"

Ted said,

"Please! Call me Ted, Mr. Robinson is my dad and he's an asshole. You don't think I'm an asshole do you- kid?

Without skipping a beat I blurted,

"No sir, not at all!"

Ted said,

"Sir? Kid I'm gonna have to whip that ass if you call me sir again. I'm not in the military."

This guy was without a doubt an A1, first class, high flying classic asshole, a lot of people are though nowadays. I was just trying to be polite to this guy. I wanted to say, go ahead and try to "*Whip this ass*" instead, I laughed and said,

"Ted! Sorry about that my friend, so what can I do for you today?"

Ted said, "I'm looking for a truck, diesel."

I said, "Of course you are Ted! You're in luck because we have the biggest selection in Denver- do you have a preference in brand?"

Ted responded, "Yeah, diesel".

I briefly acknowledged his stupidity with a slight head nod and said, "Follow me Ted, I've got a bunch to show you!"

He followed me outside to the lot where his big dumb brown eyes widened as they glazed over at the sight of line up of trucks. I turned to him and said,

"You have a preference in color?"

Ted said,

"I want me one of them red Supermaxs!"

I pointed four trucks down in the line to a red Supermax as I said,

"Like that one?"

Ted said,

"Oh yeah, just like that one"

We walked towards the behemoth diesel guzzler together, my eyes focused on the truck's sticker pasted on the passenger side window as I quickly internalized the facts and figures. He walked around the truck with his left arm outstretched as he ran his hand gently around the body of it, as if he were caressing a horse. Ted blurted, "How much?"

I responded, "Thirty-eight-five!"

Trying not to act sticker shocked he said, "I could do that... I could do that..."

"Only thirty-thousand miles on it, it's a 2019- it's actually a great price for a 2019 in this condition." I said. He quipped back, "Can we take it on a test drive?"

I said, "Sure thing, I'll just need your license and proof of insurance. I'll grab a quick copy of them and then we can hit the open road and test it out!"

He begrudgingly dug into the front right pocket of his Dockers fumbling around in search for his wallet, assumingly past a key ring because I heard the familiar clacking of bronze and other cheap metals. After a few moments he produced a tattered black leather wallet that was entirely too big; he took out his license and handed it to me while saying, "I got my insurance card on my phone, let me pull it up".

We stood there for at least two minutes until he could track it down presumably in a sea of emails.

"I got it, I got it!" He yelled.

I snapped a picture of it with my phone and told him thanks before turning around to head back to the sales floor. Over my shoulder, just for reassurance to this guy I blurted,

"I'll make a quick copy of these and be right back, SIR!"

This time I was trying to get under his skin, especially because at this point I knew that he was wasting my time. He's just like most people that go on test drives- he wasn't going to buy anything. I'm pretty sure he couldn't afford a cheeseburger, let alone this overpriced truck. When I swung open the old sun faded glass door to the sales floor I was immediately confronted by Bob who had been standing inside watching me interact with Ted the whole time through the floor to ceiling windows that were in desperate need of some Windex. I tried to give him a fake smile and a nod before attempting to squeeze by him but he side stepped right in front of me blocking my path to the photocopier. The stale coffee in his mug sloshed side to side with his quick movement as it brimmed over the top and dripped effervescently onto the floor, he pretended not to feel it all over his hairy hand or even hear the splash that it made when it hit the ground as he said, "Well... no sales today yet Walker? Huh?"

"Not yet Bob, I'm working on it." I said

He let out a bellowing laugh and exclaimed, "When I was your age, I used to have five sales a day, everyday. You're lucky to get five sales a month, you need to work the phones and sell more aggressively- you know? Raul, Darious, or even Scott all have double your numbers."

"I know Bob, thanks for the tip." I said

He looked me over from head to toe and said, "You better

make this damn sale Walker. I can get anyone to sell better than you can... you know that I can fire you right now if I wanted to. That would be a shame for you and the wife of yours... Ariel or whatever right?"

With my jaw clenched I murmured through my teeth, "I know Bob, I know- and her name is Alondra, you know that."

He pompously retorted, "Whatever, it doesn't matter, she's married to a loser. She knows it, I know it, everyone in Denver knows it. She's too good for you Walker- and you know it."

I said, "Thanks, can I copy these and take this guy on a test drive now?"

He looked down at the spilled coffee on the floor and then back into my eyes, "Sure, but after you clean up this mess."

I walked to the desk and got some paper towels to wipe up his spill- he watched me as I got them. Then he hovered over me as I proceeded to clean up the mess, without moving he unveiled an ear to ear grin on his face and said, "Get used to that Walker..."

Damn I hated this power hungry car slinging oligarch; I made copies of Ted's license and insurance and hastily headed out of the same main doors that I came in from. Ted was impatiently waiting at the truck, as soon as I emerged he yelled out, "Took you long enough huh!?"

I said, "Sorry about that Ted." before being close enough to him to outstretch my arm, almost as if it were an olive branch to him with his license in my hand. He lurched towards me as he angrily snatched it from my hand. Still trying to close a sale that I knew was dead, instead of slapping him in the mouth I smiled and said, "Ted, I talked to my sales manager while I was in there and I can get you free upgraded floor mats if you do decide to buy."

He ripped open the truck door and said, "Damn right you

can, that's the least you can do for me after keeping me waiting like that."

He had been waiting less than five minutes, again, I swallowed my pride and plastered the dealer plate on the back of the truck before getting in the passenger seat and buckling up my seatbelt.

I said, "Of course Ted- anything for you! I'm sorry about that wait- but you're going to love the way that this truck drives. It's smooth because of the dual rear suspension, you're going to feel like you're floating in a cloud!"

He begrudgingly let out a moan as he started it up and began to drive us off of the lot.

I asked, "So, are you married?" in an attempt to kindle a conversation.

Ted said, "Are you dumb? Relax with all the questions, damn! Just sit there and be quiet, if I want to know something I'll ask! But I already know everything about trucks so there ain't nothing you can tell me kid!".

I sat in silence, not wanting to participate in any pointless banter with this guy. The test drive was a lot like all of the other ones I've done in the sense that it was awkward and a complete waste of time. After we got back to the lot, just as I had suspected, he did not buy the truck. Instead he smugly tossed the keys at me and said, "You should get a real job, loser. I'm gonna buy that same truck from the place across the street.".

Fighting the urge to yell obscenities at this guy I watched as he got into his old sun stained yellow dilapidated truck and sped away before I bent over to pick up the truck keys that fell in front of me. I didn't want to give that guy the satisfaction of watching me pick them up because then I really would have looked like a defenseless loser.

Not wanting to be berated by Bob, I decided to meander around the lot for the rest of my shift which at this point was only about forty-five minutes at best. I paced up and down the lines of cars with a yellow legal pad in one hand and a blue pen in the other that I would use to pretend as if I was jotting notes down about every other car I approached. No sales again today meant that I made about sixty bucks for the day from my hourly wage after Uncle Sam took his cut. For me, this day was just like every other one- which was exactly the problem. In the back of my mind I could seemingly feel the monotony of my life gnawing at me with it's thin razor sharp claws, it was burrowing further and further into my psyche. Almost as if it was an inconvenient paper-cut at first, but then continued to have the scar burst open hourly in the same interdigital spot on your hand until it eventually got to the bone and continued to slowly saw through in a dull lingering pain that vibrated throughout your entire musculoskeletal structure. To say that I was tired would be a gross understatement, I was exhausted from expending all of my time and energy into something that I didn't care about- something that had no true meaning or impact on the world. Yet I did it day in and day out- wasting my invaluable time with menial inconsequential tasks all in pursuit of the almighty dollar. My train of thought was interrupted abruptly from an unexpected vibrating in my left front pants pocket, which for a millisecond made me jump from my skin until I remembered that it was just my phone. I dived into my pocket to see who was calling, it was Alondra. I thumbed the green button radiating on the screen to accept the call and brought the phone to my ear as I said, "Hey baby! What's up?"

"Oh nothing much really, just about to get off of work." she said

I pulled back my phone to glance at the time, "It is about three huh? That went pretty fast; how's your day been?"

She responded, "Good good, just been directing calls and

taking messages pretty much all day. What about you? Sell any cars?"

I said, "It's been... a day... no sales, Bob is still being a d-bag and I had a customer from hell. But he wasn't even a customer since he didn't buy a damned thing! He basically just belittled me and wasted my time for at least a good two hours. I hate this job babe, we need to get the hell out of this town."

She consolingly retorted, "I'm sorry baby, at least you got to get out of the sales room for a bit and away from Bob- that's always a plus. What time are you going to be home?"

I said, "Well it's time for Bob's afternoon poop so I'm going to clock out and leave now so that I don't have to run into him again. So I should be home in about thirty minutes... well if traffic doesn't suck. What time are you done?"

She said, "I'm off at three-thirty! What do you want to do for dinner tonight?"

Pausing for a moment I thought before responding, "I don't know babe; I think I'm going to drink my dinner tonight... What sounds good to you?"

She said, "Babe! You have to eat something! Chinese food sounds good, you want that?"

I said, "Sure, that sounds good- you want me to get it on my way home?"

She quickly responded, "No babe, there's that one place we like right by work, I'll swing by and get it on my way home - oh I'm getting another call, I have to go! I'll see you soon- love you!"

I said, "Okay babe, love you too!" then heard the dial tone beep of the call being ended. Knowing that Bob was a man of routine I knew that I still had a solid five minutes to clock out before he would be out of the bathroom, even so though, I didn't want to waste any time. I hastily made my way back inside and went straight to the old derelict break room - if you could even call it that. It was a ten by ten foot room with the white walls adorned with crappy motivational posters. In the right corner of the room was a soda vending machine which was notorious for stealing at least one quarter per transaction. Catty corner to that, stood a stained coffee table that might as well only have had three legs because of how damn wobbly the thing was. On the back wall was the punch clock, which was clearly from the eighties. I don't understand why they even make us use it- especially since it's twenty-twenty-one! I think they purposely enjoy demeaning us and think that they're saving a few bucks by still using it. Or maybe it's just a case of 'This is how it's always been so this is how it will always be. It's business as usual'. There's nothing more dangerous in this world than that type of archaic thinking- there's nothing more dangerous than 'business as usual'.

After clocking out I discreetly made my way to my old beat up Nissan Maxima to make my last escape of the day. I got in the car and rested my forehead on the steering wheel in a visible manifestation of my internal defeat as I used the keys jingling in my hand to stab at the ignition. I got it on the first try with the right key simply because I've felt the key in my sweaty palms a million times; I've started this car a million times- everything at this point is sheer muscle memory. A sigh escaped my lungs as I viciously turned the key with my thumb and forefinger which instantly initiated a thick rattling of gears that brought my mechanical heap of trash to life in a series of putters and metal clanking noises. Sweating from the summer heat, I reached for the crank to manually unroll my window so that I didn't have to gasp at the sun heated oven hot air that was locked inside surrounding me before I backed up and drove out of the lot. With the window down but still sweating I drove home in complete silence- my car's tape deck was broken and the radio only vomited static noise at me because it had no antenna or maybe because it was 30 years old- most likely it was a combination of both. My car's air conditioning had never worked either but at this point I was indifferent to it. What I had still not learned to be indifferent to was traffic, which is what I now found myself stuck in. Aloud to myself I murmured an observation that manifested in my mind, "I live in Hell. I LIVE IN HELL!".

Forty-five minutes later I had finally arrived back home to my apartment; when I stepped out of my car my undershirt which was soaking wet had bled through my other shirt so that both fused to my back and stuck to my car seat too. Before closing the car's door I stared briefly but intently at the silhouette of me that was sweat etched into the seat knowing that tomorrow my car was not going to smell like a dozen fresh roses. I walked two minutes from where I was able to find parking to my apartment's front door; without even looking at my keys I felt the one I knew was the right one and gingerly slipped it into the lock's patterned brass opening. I could feel the pins of the lock move up into the mechanism as they all aligned just enough so that the key could turn allowing the apparatus to roll and manipulate the bolt into an open position. As I opened the door I noticed that the white ocean spray scented candle in the middle of our kitchen island was not yet lit. Alondra does this everyday as soon as she gets home so I knew she wasn't there yet. I closed the front door as I kicked off my cheap black imitation leather loafers. I also removed all of my sweaty clothes and just left them there in the entryway before grabbing a quick shower. The cold water felt so damn refreshing; after I dried off I threw on an old pair of shorts, grabbed a beer from the refrigerator and settled into the couch as I cracked it open and listened to the carbonation hiss its way from the can before taking a long draw from it. The frigid beer was even better than the shower, it was exactly what I needed. I sat there staring at the stained beige tinged wall in our living room silently with the exception of the upstairs neighbors who must have been wearing brick clogs-

that's the only way that they could have been making so much damned noise up there. I also could faintly hear coughing which was an indicator that our neighbor in apartment B-Twenty-Two was home and that soon I would catch the nightly waft of his exhaled pot smoke even though all of our windows were shut. The echoes of kids screaming also bounced off of the apartment buildings and carried throughout the hallways- I guess the only true silence was in my mind and it was only a hope for silence- it wasn't real. Half out of enjoyment and half stemming from disdain I gulped the rest of my golden colored ale and tossed the can on the floor in defiance before getting up to grab another. Just as I opened up the refrigerator Alondra appeared in the doorway as it swung open with a heavy push, holding a bag of Chinese food in her right hand and her car keys in the other. She put both on the kitchen island before lighting the white ocean spray candle, kissing me in an embraceful hug, and going about the same end of day ritual of showering. When she emerged from showering we ate dinner on the couch while we talked about our days, watched the news, drank, and watched more T.V... I love her, I love our life together- but again, it was more of the same. We did the same thing everyday- eventually we passed out on the couch then migrated to bed before brushing our teeth, taking turns using the same sink. I wanted two sinks, I wanted somewhere quiet to live, I wanted a better job, I wanted to travel, I wanted us to have an exciting life... I wanted... we dozed off to bed for an escape from reality in our dreams. Everything we wanted was a dream, all of it out of our grasp.

PURGATORY

I awoke from a dead sleep in a cold sweat, the time on my feeble blinking alarm clock displayed 05:30 A.M. in a fluorescent red glare- I rolled over in dismay in an attempt to avoid what imminent truth was about to be revealed. Today was Tuesday morning, I'm now officially late for work- my cycle continued. We went about our brief morning routines before leaving each other to part ways for work for the day. I was the one responsible for opening up the sales floor everyday Monday through Friday. This consisted of unlocking the main doors, putting on a pot of stale coffee for Bob so that it was ready by the time he strolls into work around nine and washing every car in the lot. Every car did not need to be washed everyday- not at all- but this was just another way for Bob to exert his power over me and try to make me quit. I would quit if I could, but I can't afford to so this is my life. It typically takes me around three hours to power-wash all the cars, today was no different. Afterwards I change clothes so that I'm in something a bit more presentable and then I man the sales desk, blinded by that same red glare of the Camaro. Today, Bob decided to show up at about nine-thirty, as usual he began to berate me, "Morning... did you clean the cars today?" he said.

I said, "I sure did Bob, just like I do every morning."

He let out a sign of disapproval as he said, "That's exactly the problem- you did it *just like you do every morning*- and you don't do it worth a shit! These cars should be shining like the sun! They need to be so damn clean that they catch people's attention! We need people to see our cars so they actually come in and BUY our cars! Are you stupid or do you just not care? Or maybe it's both?"

Gritting my teeth I said, "I do care Bob- the cars are clean. I'm not an idiot, but you are, especially if you think that you can keep talking to me like that! You can't put on a cheap suit and fake jewelry and think that you're someone. I haven't lost my temper yet but it would be a shame if I did and I beat the shit out you wouldn't it? Next time you spill coffee maybe I'll grab a fist full of that greasy ass hair and use you to mop it up!"

Taken aback he slammed his coffee on the desk and tried to interject, "I don't know who you think you're..."

I sprung up from my chair and batted his coffee cup off the desk, "Shut your mouth Bob! Before you say another damned word you better listen and listen closely! I'm a person, and you're going to treat me like one! No more of this bull-shit! Any more and I'll tell that wife of yours about that blonde girl you always have in your office on Wednesdays- I know what you're doing in there- WE all know! You try to fire me or even think about disrespecting me or any of us then you will be out of a job because your wife will take this place in your divorce!"

His face turned bright red as he searched for something to say, "I... you... you..."

Again I cut him off, "You are going to clean up that damn mess, and I'm going to sell some cars! Not another word- get a towel and hurry up- I don't want any of our customers to slip."

I fully expected to be fired at that exact moment, I had no idea what he was going to do or say. I stood my ground without saying another word just staring into his eyes showing him through my clenched fists and demeanor that the ball was in his court and if he was feeling froggy then it was damned time to leap! He too stood there and knew that I was not bluffing, his breathing became heavier and his face even more flushed as he swiped his hair, pasting it back to his head without saying another word. He walked to the break room and came back carrying a single roll of paper towels, he got on his hands and knees and began to clean up the mess. I sat back down and watched as he did so- it was tense, the air felt heavy and I felt unsure of my actions because my whole paycheck- my livelihood was this. Unexpectedly I heard the unmistakable bell from the front door knell but at a pitch that was lower and I felt the sound of it reverberate from the walls and inside of my chest. I looked up from Bob to see a man standing in the front entryway draped in an unrecognizably old suit. It was definitely a suit - but it seemed to be from another era or time. It was a deep tan color with pants that were high-waisted, almost to his nipples it seemed. The pants themselves were very wide-legged yet tightly-cuffed at the ankles and the jacket looked more like a long coat with wide lapels. Even more confusing was the jacket's wide padded shoulders that made this man in his twenties appear bigger than he truly was - he just looked so out of place standing there with that slightly cockeyed fedora polishing off his whole look. His eyes darted across the room as if it were the first time he'd ever seen anything, like everyone else though his gaze was eventually fixed on the red Camaro. I stood up from my chair and exclaimed, "Zoot suit riot! She's beautiful right? I'm Walker Henderson, how can I help you?"

The man hauntingly looked through Bob and then up at me, "What are you talking about?" he desperately exclaimed.

I said, "It's a joke- you know the uhhhh- Zoot Suit Riots? LA, nineteen-forty-three..."

The man walked up to Bob and kicked him directly in the mouth with the heel of his black Oxford dress shoes! The vicious kick rendered Bob instantly unconscious as his torso slumped to the tiled floor in a thundering plop- his head banged against the floor once before rebounding again from the sheer force and coming to a rest in the pooled coffee! I could hear the clatter of his freshly removed teeth jingle as they skipped across the floor in a bright red trail of blood before coming to a morbid rest a few mere inches from my feet!

I yelled out in shock, "Jesus! What did you do that for! Relax man! What do you..."

Cutting me off the man shouted, "Pipe down fella!" as he swiped away the right side of his blazer to reveal the steel handle of a gun tucked in his waistband! He removed the gun with his oddly steady hand and brandished it in my direction as he assumed a wide legged shooting stance! I was staring down the barrel of the thing as my hands instinctively shot up towards the ceiling! In a stale calm voice he said, "Listen fella, I can't kill you but I can hurt you real bad. Now you're going to do exactly what I say or I'm gonna put some holes in you with this forty-five."

I exclaimed, "Don't shoot, put it down, I'll do whatever you want! There's a safe in the back, I can open it for..."

Interjecting he said, "Pipe down! I don't want your money! I need a Willys! I'm late- I need a Willys! Get me one right now!"

Fumbling over my words I said, "Willys? What are you talking about! Look we don't have to get weird here, I don't know what you're into but come on man leave my chocolate factory alone..."

Raising his voice he shouted, "Damn it! A Willy Jeep! Do you have one or not! I'm late! I need a Willys JEEP! We need to go now!"

Still confused, I conceded, "We have some Jeep's out back, I'll take you to them!"

With the gun still fixed on me he nodded in approval and said, "Well let's go! No funny business fella! I'll put some holes in you I swear to Christ I will! Get the keys and let's go!"

I said, "Alright- alright! The keys are in this drawer! I'm just going to open it to grab the keys and then we can go!"

I opened the desk drawer and dove in it with my right hand while leaving my left hand up towards the ceiling in a signal of my compliance. My hands were both shaking in a hysterical fear, I was freezing up, I felt like I couldn't grip the keys- it was as if the dexterity of my hand was that of Gumby's. I looked back up at the man to see that he now had a pocket watch in his left hand which is what his eyes were transfixed on, even though he still had the gun pointed at me with his other. Then I felt a stinging pain in both of my ears that caused an instant mind numbing ringing! I felt an explosive pulse of energy reverberate throughout my chest and the whiz of a focused stream of air push past my head that dropped me to the floor clutching my ears in pain! Adrenaline coursed through my veins as in that instant I realized that what I just felt was a bullet careening through the air past my head!

"Shit! What the hell!" I cried out in horror! The ringing in my ears muffled the way that my voice sounded aloud!

The man yelled out, "The next one won't be over your head! We need to GO NOW!"

It sounded as if he were yelling in a tunnel, everything was muffled- my eyes were blurred, my heart was skipping beats as it relentlessly thudded in my chest! Before I knew it the man was on top of me, he ripped me up angrily by the arm and pressed the barrel of the gun to the side of my head! It was scorching hot from the last shot so as it made contact to my right temple it instantly burned me! I cried out, "Stop- please! FUCK"! The thick smell of the gun powder and my own sizzling flesh carried throughout the stale air and buried itself in my lungs! I was brought to my feet still in a complete state of disarray, I grabbed a handful of the car keys and he forcibly escorted me outside the main doors with the gun now dug into my back.

He said, "Right or left"?

"Right!" I cried out! Stumbling over myself I walked to where the Jeeps were in the lot and said, "Here these are the Jeeps! Take 'em all- take whatever you want!"

He said, "What! This is not a Jeep! What the hell is this contraption! This is no Willys! DAMN IT! I said no funny business!"

He shoved me against the hood of the car and buried the barrel of the forty-five into my neck! He said, "I can't drive this damned thing!"

Pleading I said, "I'll drive! I'll take you wherever you want to go! Just don't shoot me!"

"Get in!" he ordered; I got in the driver's seat, he got in the passenger's seat. He kept the gun fixed on me as he ordered, "Take me to Union Station! I need to catch the train to get to the Demolition Bombing Range with the rest of my squadron! We're shipping out this afternoon!"

In his left hand emerged the same pocket watch as before, he stared at it intently watching the sweeping second hand tick with an impatience that I've never before witnessed.

I said, "Okay- Union Station." and began to drive. This man seemed entirely out of his mind, everything was new to him- it was as if he was from another time. Everything about the guy made me uneasy in a way that I'd never felt before. Obviously I was scared shitless, but his presence is what made me the most uncomfortable. I had no idea what he was talking about, I knew that there was no such thing as a Demolition Bombing Range, the closest military base to us was Buckley Air Force Base in Aurora but still, you can't get to the base by train. I began to merge onto the main interstate, I-25, heading south towards downtown Denver nonetheless. The man's eyes were still transfixed on the watch and his knuckles turned white from his death grip on his pistol. From the corner of my eye I could tell that it was a .45 caliber Colt 1911 that he was holding me hostage with. Without even looking at me he said, "What do you mean there's no Demolition Bombing Range? What's Buckley Air Force Base? Why can't I get there from Union Station?"

Taken aback I said, "What? I never said that? You said to take you to Union Station man and that's exactly what I'm doing".

My voice in the back of my head told me that everything was going to be okay- in an eerie calm, I believed it, I knew it in my bones. I thought to myself that I should just tell him exactly what I was thinking and somehow I felt some sort of reassurance that there would be no retribution for doing so. I continued, "There's no such thing as the Demolition Bombing Range, the closest military base to us now is Buckley, it would take us about thirty minutes to get there from here, but even so- you're going to be late. The 336th Airborne is already shipped out- we're late.". He lowered the gun and an indelible smile curved his thin lips up towards his ears as he said, "Now you know- that voice in your head is mine. I hear your thoughts, I'm inside your head Walker. You know why we're here."

Any remaining color I had in my face immediately drained as I exclaimed, "What the hell? What the..." my inner voice told me not to panic, again reassuring me that everything was fine. The man tucked his Colt back into his waistband as he rocked his head back into the seat and exhaled a deep sigh before saying, "We still need to go to Union Station. We are going to catch that train, Walker.

Without even thinking I blurted, "Dwight, we're going to be there in time- but it's going to be tight... wait... how do I know your name? How do I know you? I know you. How in the hell do I know you?"

He said,

"I'm in your head. Your thoughts are mine, your feelings are my feelings- there is no you and I anymore- there's just we, us."

Then he used his thumb and forefinger to wind the shining metal crown of the pocket watch in his hand. First I heard the distinct mechanical click of gears turning the mechanisms of the watch's movement. Then my mind was flooded with memories that were not mine but were lived through my eyes- my mind became inundated with all of them. Each click of the watch seemed to impress a memory of Dwight's into my brain, it overcame my consciousness. Within a mere second or two I knew everything about Dwight, I felt like I was him. His birthday was July seventh, nineteen twenty-one, he was the youngest of four children- his parents are Marguerite and Clyde, they both immigrated to America from Cosenza Italy in nineteen-eighteen. They were both farmers in Welby Colorado, they were poor but scrapped by- mainly by selling asparagus and alfalfa at the local Denver swap meets. Dwight enlisted in the army the day after the attacks at Pearl Harbor, he was an Army pilot in the 336th Airborne Squadron and had completed basic training at the Demolition Bombing Range. He was chosen by the Office of Strategic Services to fly B-17s in missions that were essential to the war effort... I knew everything.

Dwight looked at me and said, "I can't explain it. I don't know why we're here. All I know is that we have to catch that train."

I was at a complete loss for words, my entire reality had been turned inside out in a matter of seconds- I began questioning my sanity. Even so, my inner voice told me to not think about it and just focus on driving, focus on getting to Union Station and then for me, all of this madness would end. Dwight pulled out a zippo lighter and a vintage pack of cigarettes before flopping one end over end with the flick of his wrist into his lips. As he sparked the flint of the zippo with his thumb he said, "I know you don't smoke- otherwise I'd offer you one. I guess smoking is bad for us? Huh- never would have thought." The paper end of the cigarette that protected the encased tobacco quickly took to the flame as the ebb and flow of his respiratory system symphonized with the death stick. The cherry of the cigarette burned a bright red as he took two deep draws of smoke and exhaled casually into the air. The thick smoke of tobacco overtook the cab- it smelled different though, it was as if it was a more botanical earthy scent as opposed to the secondhand smoke that I'm accustomed to breathing in from others. That smoke had a deep lingering metal tingle outlined by a trailing tar taste that you could almost feel deep inside your throat as your body viciously fought off the idea of allowing the substance to be absorbed into you. Nonetheless, I didn't like the smell of either so I rolled down the window. As it began to recede itself into the door frame Dwight was startled, "What the hell! What's it doing?"

I said, "Relax, I'm just cracking the windows so that I can breathe."

He said, "Wow- no cranks no nothing huh? I guess I'm a real fuddy-duddy around here huh?"

I didn't feel like responding because all my focus was on the road. My inner voice told me I needed to go faster- I needed to get there no matter what. My foot pressed the gas pedal to the floor in a desperate angst as I weaved through the sporadic traffic that was slowing us down on I-25 until we got to our exit on Park Avenue. I was driving way too damned fast, I knew it, but I couldn't stop myself! I knew that we were getting close, I blazed through a red light at Wewatta Street where Delgany Street intersected with 22nd Avenue- I knew I messed up before I even saw it. I felt my heart sink into my stomach and adrenaline coarse through my veins in a perilous fight or flight animalistic reaction! The inner voice told me to crank the wheel to the left- my consciousness conveyed that there was a red car barreling towards our passenger side even though I'd still not seen it, Dwight did. He let out a hoarse low pitched moan, "Nooooo!" then I heard the unmistakable crunch of metal as the red car careened into ours, I felt the left side of my head bury itself into the driver side window which instantly shattered- then my eyes faded to a deep sea of black.

When I regained consciousness the haunting echo of the Jeep's horn was blaring- directly stoking the fire of the intense throbbing pain in my head. I tried to look to my right to check if Dwight was alright but moving my neck in any manner shot a numbing pain that radiated from the base of my head to all the way through my spine. He wasn't in the passenger seat any longer- the entire passenger side of the Jeep's was completely caved inward in a concave heap of metal. I unfastened my seat-belt and pushed down the airbag before trying the door handle in a feeble attempt to get out of the car. I was fully expecting that the door wouldn't budge, but it opened without a prob-lem. The engine of the Jeep was fuming a thick grey smoke that added to my disillusionment but I still looked around for Dwight. Wiping away the warm red blood oozing from my forehead out of my eyes I could only see a scattered mess of debris from the collision. Noticing that the rear driver's side window was completely shattered I looked into the back seat, I saw a body heaped over in the shape of an uppercase 'U'. It was Dwight's body laying motionless- what remained of his stomach was the curve of the 'U' that was pressed against the door, he was completely upside down so that his legs were dangling on top of him. His torso was the bottom of the 'U' his spine was snapped in half - it protruded from his stomach surrounded by his entrails. There was blood everywhere, I was in complete disbelief of what I was looking at, I've never seen a human so terribly mangled it didn't look real. None of this felt like it was even within the realm of possibilities yet here I was staring at this ghastly sight. I was in an utter state of shock, I felt my body with both my hands to check that all of my appendages were still attached. I felt exceedingly relieved that they were, I was just really banged up. I hobbled over to the other side of the Jeep to see the car that hit us. Slumped over the steering wheel, the car's airbag was half deflated supporting the head of a person bleeding profusely but not moving at all. I yelled out to him, "You alright? HEY! ARE YOU OKAY?" Even though I already knew the answer. I had the wherewithal to try to call the police to report the accident, I frisked my pockets looking for my phone but it wasn't there. I leaned into what was the passenger side window of the Jeep to see if it was inside- it wasn't. The only thing that caught my eye was something gleaming in a bright silver glow from the midday sun on the floor. Climbing half into the car I palmed at it with my hand trying to get it- I did. The thick blood coating my hands dampened it's shine once I emerged from the Jeep with it in my palm. It was Dwight's pocket watch, it had an unexpected weight to it. It's face was adorned with three white sweeping clock hands that stood a stark contrast to its black background which was emboldened with two rings of white numbers. The inner ring of numbers had the number twenty-four in the place of where twelve would usually be on a regular clock, then it went around in numerical order so that it depicted military time. The outer ring of numbers was painted in increments of five minutes starting with the number sixty directly above the number twenty-four with a horizontal white notch annotated for each minute. It was still working, I could feel the movement of the gears tick steadily in my palm with each second that propelled the sweeping second hand almost more vividly than my own pulse. Something inside of me told me that I needed this watch, I wanted it, it had to be mine... I stashed it in my pocket before recognizing the familiar glare of the red car that was sandwiched into the Jeep. I looked up in shock, it was a red Camaro- I thought to myself that there was no way that this was the same car as in our sales room, it was an impossibility! Even so, I needed to check to be sure, I stumbled to the back of the Camaro where my suspicions were confirmed! It has the same dealer plaque template in the license slot as the one back in the sales room! Out of sheer exhaustion, pain, and fear I collapsed to the ground.

OUR NIGHTMARES

My eyelids worked as curtains in perfect synchronicity to uncover my eyes which instantly exposed them to a bright white light encased in the middle by speckled white and black ceiling tiles that ended at the top corner of a solid surgical white wall. I knew immediately that I was in a hospital room- I knew I wasn't dead yet because every inch of my body was radiating in a pain I could tell was being dulled by some sort of opiate. I could hear the steady ding of the medical apparatuses connected to me making my pulse electronically audible. I slowly lifted my head to survey the room, Alondra was there, I tried to speak, "Hey baby, how are you..."

She said, "Walker! Oh my God! I'm so glad that you're okay! What happened?"

Only half joking I asked, "Am I okay? I... I'm not sure what happened- I was hoping that you could tell me".

"You were in a bad car accident! The person you were on a test drive with passed away!" she exclaimed.

I quipped, "I remember that part, but he kidnapped me- we weren't on a test drive."

She said, "What? He kidnapped you? Baby you're twenty-seven years old... wouldn't that be like man-napped?"

I let out a laugh and said, "Baby I'm serious, I really got kidnapped. Call the dealership, I'm pretty sure the guy broke Bob's jaw too; it was crazy! I'm sure that there's got to be a police report filed if Bob is still alive".

She said, "Baby you do have a concussion and your collarbone is broken- so you have to rest. I believe you but what's important is that you rest right now. I love you, we're so lucky that you're okay."

I said, "I love you too! Do you have my phone or my clothes? Where is all my stuff?"

She gestured to a clear trash bag across the room on a chair containing all my belongings as she said, "They couldn't find your phone but your clothes and wallet are all in there."

All I could think about was that pocket watch- I needed it. I casually asked, "Can you bring me the bag? Or at least just my pants."

She said, "Yeah- what do you need? Your wallet?"

"No- just hand me my pants if you could." I said

She said, "Sure, but you're not putting them on and walking out of here if that's what you're thinking."

She rifled through the bag briefly before tossing them to me in a balled up heap. As the bloodied pants landed in my lap I could feel the weight of the watch in the pocket; I immediately tried to orient them right-side up draped over my lap so that I could get inside and grab it.

"Thank you." I said - as my hand cupped the cold metal back of the watch in my palm and secured it with my fingertips. I felt a sudden rush of cheap gratification, almost as if my brain released a quick jolt of serotonin in my body; I felt better than I had just moments ago.

Alarmingly Alondra said, "Whoa, are you okay?"

I said, "Yeah, I'm fine- why?"

She said, "Your pupils just dilated to the entire size of your iris! It was like your eyes were nothing but pupils! I can see it now- they're shrinking down to normal."

Reassuringly I said, "That's the morphine drip baby... pull up a chair and let me see your arm, we got to get you some of this shit -it's good!"

She flashed me a grin while shaking her head, "It must be! That was bizarre."

I knew that it was the watch that had the effect on me, not morphine, but how could I tell her that without her thinking I was crazy. I used the watch to segway the conversation- "Babe not everything was bad today though, I found this cool pocket watch." I said as I produced it from my pants pocket and into her view.

She said, "That is a silver lining... damn, that is actually pretty cool! What is it?"

I said, "It is! I have no idea what it is, it's an antique watch of some sort. I found it in one of the cars today."

She said, "It might be worth some money! Let me see it."

I thought to myself: *don't let her touch it, don't let anyone touch it- it's yours! Tell her that it's covered in blood so she can't touch it! Wind it...wind it... WIND IT!*

I said, "Nah, it's covered in blood babe, it's nasty. I'll have to wipe it off first." as I slowly began to wind the crown of it counterclockwise.

She said, "Babe! Your eyes- they're doing it again! Should I call in the doctor? Maybe it's your concussion- can you even have pain meds with a concussion? I think it's too much babe!"

I snapped back at her, "It's fine! I'm fine - just relax. Just relax with me babe it's been... a day."

She reluctantly rolled her big beautiful hazel eyes at me as she conceded to my request by agreeing with me through silence. She scooted the cheap faux burgundy leather reclining chair that she was sitting in up to the left side of my bed and firmly grasped my hand.

"I love you, I'm glad you're okay. I don't know what I would do without you." she said

I said, "I love you more- me either, so we have to stay together."

I kept the watch gripped in my right hand under the hospital bed sheets almost as firm as I held onto Alondra's hand until I drifted off into a semi-conscious half asleep state.

I was roused back to consciousness by a female voice gently calling out my name, it was presumably a nurse, "Walker... Walker?" the voice said. My eyes followed my still ringing ears to the sound of the voice emanating from the doorway. My suspicions were confirmed, it was a nurse, she was wearing purple scrubs, she had her blonde hair expertly pinned up. She was standing next to a man who had a badge and a gun attached to his belt so I assumed he was a cop.

"Yes" I said

She said, "I'm Sara, it's nice to meet you. I'm the on call nurse for the rest of the evening for this unit. This is Detective Torrez, he has some questions for you. Are you feeling well enough to talk?"

"Yeah, that's fine with me." I said

"Okay, well let me know if you need anything, you can just press that little 'call' button on that remote." She said

I cordially replied, "Thank you!"

As soon as the nurse exited the room, Detective Torres said, "Well, as she mentioned, I'm Detective Torres- I wish we could have met under different circumstances but here we are. So I spoke to your manager Bob, what exactly happened?"

Hesitantly I began to recount what had occurred, "Well, it all happened so fast. Bob and I had gotten into an argument because... well... the guy is a dick man, there's no two ways about it. After our little argument, Bob was cleaning up his spilled coffee when this guy came in; I mean he looked really odd but I figured he was just another weird customer- we get a lot of them around here. Anyway, he booted Bob right in the mouth and then he pulled a gun out on me! He demanded that I give him a Jeep, then that bastard shot at me! It was like a warning shot right over my head, I felt the bullet whiz by! Then that prick burned me with the barrel of his gun- look you can see it right here on my head! He kept saying *"I'll fill you full of holes."* or some kind of threat like that and saying that he was late for something - the guy was out of his damn mind. I brought him to our Jeep inventory then he demanded that I drive him to Union Station, he kept the gun pointed at me so I did exactly what he said. I was driving him to Union Station and I was scared shitless, then we got into an accident and all I remember is waking up here."

Detective Torres said, "That sounds like a very traumatic experience- I'm sorry that you had to go through that. As you may or may not know, the suspect died in the accident that you were in. That being said, we have great camera footage of him from the dealership and we're currently trying to establish his identity. Did you know the suspect or have you ever seen him around the dealership before?"

I said, "No sir- I have no idea who that guy was! I have never seen him before in my life!"

Both of those statements were true, but since I had all of Dwight's memories drilled into my mind it felt weird saying it.

Detective Torres said, "Any idea why he would target you- or that car dealership? Do you have any enemies?"

I said, "No idea, I don't have any enemies."

He said, "Well again- I'm sorry you've experienced this. If there's anything I can do to help or if you think of anything else you may have forgotten- just give me a call... oh and do you need the assistance of a Victim's Advocate."

I said, "No, no, no- I'm fine, I'll be okay. I'll definitely give you a call if I think of anything, thanks for your help!"

He outstretched his business card to me and I accepted it with a nod before he turned around and walked out of my room. Alondra was still sitting next to me, the brief conversation hadn't woken her, she was still in a deep sleep. The chaos of the day replayed inside of my mind on repeat but my memory was clouded with Dwight's too. Vicariously through him, I watched- I participated in a variety of B-17 bombing raids mostly over Germany- I think. All the memories were there but some of the details were just out of my grasp, I couldn't see them as vividly as I had the first time that they were etched into my mind. I knew the overall details as to what we were doing in each raid or who each person was through his eyes- but I couldn't decipher the little things anymore. I had no desire to have any of these thoughts or shared memories- yet they circled my consciousness; with a morbid curiosity it felt like an itch that I just had to scratch. Almost as if I had tourettes, it's my mind, my body, but the memories and thoughts inside of me were dictated by something in my head that I had zero control over.

I conceded to the now unbearable weight of my eyelids and restlessness of my beaten body as I drifted off into a true uninterrupted sleep. Through a dirty pair of flight goggles I could see perspiration of breath emanating from the progressively increasing discords of inhales and exhales from a body that I was inside of. I was wearing a tattered brown leather jacket adorned with flight patches on both the left arm and the right chest that read *316th Airborne* next to our insignia of a Bald Eagle holding a bomb in its talons with both its wings outstretched. The Flying Fortress's roaring engines were loud enough to cloak the whistle of air entering and exiting through the various bullet holes in the plane's dark green skin. The briskness of the breeze along with the glimpses of moonlight dancing off the ocean through the misshapen gaps- were more than enough to make their presences known. Uncle Sam had put this plane through the ringer- I'm not sure how it could still possibly be suspended amongst the fickle night sky clouds- but there we were. The eyes that I was peering through were that of the Bombadier's. His name was Wesley Freeman- I was somehow in his head. My thoughts were dictated to me separately but I could influence his actions through altering his cognitive thoughts. Wesley was increasingly nervous, in his head I told him, "... *relax, everything is going to be okay. Everything is going to be okay. We are not going to get shot down, we are going to open the bomb bay once we're over Hamburg. Just like we talked about in our briefing, it's a military target. We have to do this... deep breaths.*". Wesley proceeded to inhale and exhale in a calmer more reassured manner.

I was his inner voice. I was his subconscious mind.

The things I said were conveyed to him in his own consciousness via his own narrative- it was as if I were an outside observer but inside the situation. I told him, *"look left"* Wesley's vision darted to the left of the bomb bay. I told him, *"your right arm itches, scratch it"*, Wesley scratched his arm accordingly. It was exactly like this in the car accident the other day when I veered the Jeep to try to avoid the collision that I somehow knew was going to happen even though I had not yet seen the threat with my own eyes. In the same manner that my inner voice was overtaken, I was now the one dictating someone else's- in this case it was Wesley.

I could hear his thoughts, he was thinking that we were five minutes out from the target site, I told him, *"ask JR how far out we are."*, sure as shit- he did exactly that! He yelled out to the Pilot, "JR- how far out are we?" JR hollered back, "We're about four minutes out! Open the bomb bay doors!"

Wesley looked down at his navigational instrument- it was the pocket watch encased in some sort of cylindrical grey painted metal housing with a gaping hole smack dab in the middle of it where the watch laid in plain view! He manipulated the notched silver crown of the watch in a manner that hacked it into some sort of stop watch with the sweeping second hand ticking away like a timer!

He yelled out to the rest of the crew, *"Opening the bomb bay doors!"*

Then he pulled a steel painted yellow lever which immediately flapped open the underbelly doors of the plane! Gusts of wind wafted through the interior with a ferociousness much fiercer than before! Wesley gazed into the watch intently counting every second as it passed, only looking away momentarily when glints of light poked through the opened doors from the ground below into his wide eyes. I felt Wesley's fear, he was scared of heights, so looking at the ground from the hole in the plane was not the most ideal situation. Luckily the queued up bombs precisely stacked in the bay blocked the majority of his view. I attempted to cajole him out of his phobia by telling him, *"Soon we will be landing back on solid ground. Everything is going to be alright. There's only two minutes until we dump the payload and head back to base. Plus if anything did go wrong there are enough parachutes hanging right there for all of us."* Wesley's thoughts combated mine, *"There's no way I can reach the parachutes in time if we're shot down. I'm going to fall out of this damned bomb bay! What if I miss the target and they're able to put more flak up? We're all as good as dead."* Not wanting to submit I pushed further, *"None of that is going to happen- we won't miss the target. We can't miss the target... We got this, it's almost done."* He still had his own free will to listen to me as his inner voice or believe his own bantering thoughts - which most likely added to his confusion and fear. I could tell that he had no idea that I was even a part of his mind even though my consciousness was omnipresently fused with his subconscious- it was absolutely bizarre but somehow I completely grasped exactly what was occurring. The stop watched ticked hauntingly until there were only a few seconds left, then he cried out to the crew, "Five... four... three... two... one... bombs away!" He hastily pulled a red lever that unlocked the main mechanism securing the bombs in place, with a clatter one-thousand times the pitch of dominos falling sequentially, the bombs unleashed in a staggered but uniform manner as they seemingly suspended themselves in the crisp night air. I watched through Wesley's eyes as they descended towards the earth in a barreling roar and out view from the hatch. A few moments later, before he even had a chance to close the bomb bay- I heard the explosion of the first few bombs as they kissed the earth in an embrace of sheer destruction. Then I felt the pressure of them thud inside his narrow chest as the shockwaves bled into the air subsequently shaking the plane. Wesley yelled out, "Bomb bay secured! JR- did we get 'em?" JR yelled back, "It sure as hell looks like it!" Suddenly Wesley's fears came to fruition as the plane was maneuvering a sharp right turn, explosions filled the air around the Flying Fortress- the shockwaves violently jutted the plane's wings up and down in the air. JR yelled out what was now obvious, "Flak! Those bastards- shit! Everyone hold on!" Now Wesley's fear was palpable in every nerve ending of both my body and his! I told him, *Pray. Get the watch from the case and pray.* Wesley hands clamored with the cold metal case housing the watch in an attempt to remove it from the housing as he prayed out loud, "Our Father, who art in heaven, hallowed be thy name; thy kingdom come; thy will be done on earth as it is in heaven. Give us this day our daily bread; and forgive us our trespasses as we forgive..." Just as he got the watch removed and safely deposited into his cargo pants pocket, flak erupted through the middle of the plane's cabin! The five men aboard the flying coffin cried out in a disturbing unison then JR hollered, "We're going down! Brace or jump!" A gaping wound in the plane bled air as three of the crew left their flight positions and tried to make their way towards the parachutes! JR stayed in the cockpit, Wesley stumbled across the plane- grabbing anything he could use as support to help make his way. The gaping hole from the flak was adjacent to where the parachutes were pinned to the plane's cabin. Wesley got as close to the hole as he could without being sucked out of the plane- that's when he saw that there were only three parachutes, the other two were lost into the dark night sky presumably still affixed to the now missing portion of the plane! He yelled out, "Shit! There's only three!" In horror, the rest of the crew were close enough to observe the same grim conclusion. Begrudgingly I made the decision for them, *"Help Darrell, Will, and Terrence get the parachutes on and make the jump. Today is our day... we will stay with the plane."* Wesley could have fought back against the self destructive influence that I implanted into his head but he didn't. He never even gave it a second thought, he yelled out to the three, "Come one, lets go! Get your chutes on! We're losing altitude quickly!"

Terrance hollered back, "There's only three! We either all jump or we all stay- that's how it's going to be!"

Wesley cupped his hand against the right side of his mouth to amplify his voice, "I have the other two parachutes at my battlestation! We're all jumping! JR and I have to dump the remaining payload and disable the radio first!"

I didn't even prompt that response- I wouldn't have even been able to think of it that quickly, especially with what we were experiencing. We both knew exactly what was about to transpire, Wesley was scared beyond words- I felt his fear in the marrow of my bones. I felt myself fighting back tears so deep inside my eyes that my sinuses pooled with mucus as the lump in my throat seemingly tripled in size. Our emotions were now bubbling over a cauldron of anxiety mixed with terror, uncertainty fused with an utter loss of hope. A true incomprehensible resignation to the bleak realization our prerogative of breath was owed to the inescapable fate- death. With a smile pasted on Wesley's colorless face his answer was quickly well received, he gave them all a reassuring nod and waved them off with his hand.

Darrell yelled, "Well hurry it up! When we get down there we're going to be surrounded by those wienerschnitzel gobbling goons!"

Wesley again hollered, "Don't worry- I still have rations of mustard!"

JR called out, "We don't have a rally point this far north! Our only shot is to make it to Denmark! Godspeed- we will see you down there!"

The other three crew got their parachutes snugly affixed to their backs as they all prepared in an unspoken hesitation for a jump that was almost certain to end in death or being captured.

Will gave a salute to Wesley as he yelled, "See you on the other side!" and took the leap of faith from the rapidly descending fortress. Staggered but in a quick orderly fashion, Terrance and Darrell too jumped out of the plane after briefly attempting to say their farewells without saying goodbye. Wesley's facade of calm exuded itself out from his body by physically manifesting itself through an uncontrollable shaking. Turbulence sent the plane into a violent one-hundred and eighty degree twist that lifted Wesley off his feet and threw his body about the cabin like a rag doll until the descending plane steadied itself more parallel to the ground while maintaining its downward trajectory. Barely avoiding being sucked out, Wesley settled himself on his hands and knees as he got his bearings now only a mere foott from the cockpit. I could feel the warm blood pool from the top of his head as vividly as I could see its bright shade of red as it flowed over his eyes and collected in a steady drip at the bridge of his narrow nose. This severely blurred our vision, I saw his hands paw at his eye sockets in an attempt to dredge the blood away just enough so that we could make out shapes. It worked well enough that he was able to crawl into the copilot's chair adjacent to JR as he settled in a heap in the seat. Without looking over JR said, "We're going to die."

Wesley remarked, "Yeah... we are. Are you scared?"

JR said, "Shitless. I've got no control of the rudders, we're at the mercy of the wind and gravity now." Then he shut off the dilapidated engines of the plane which were all but useless at this point. The two men sit in silence with the exception of the haunting whistle of the metal beast gliding through the air as they come to terms with their imminent fate. Wesley cycled through his mind shuffling his memories in a rapid fire projected into the back of his eyes. So much life lived in so little time- yet so much was inevitably to be missed which was the second hardest part of leaving this world. He would never be married. He would never have the grandchildren that his mother and father had hoped for. He would never live out his dream of owning that surf shop on Ventura City Beach that he so desperately yearned for. Never again would he smell the simple damp crispness of a warm summer rain as it's essence joined the earth's soil to radiate that oh so familiar smell. He would never see his brother, sister, parents, his hopeful wife Marguerite who had always toyed with his heart... so much of life would be lost. Out of everything Wesley did feel, the one thing he didn't, was regret. The odd macabre sense of peace that overtook us both was truly unbelievable; how we could experience both perilous dread and blissful peace simultaneously is something that my mind couldn't grasp. I watched as our vision came closer and closer to the ground- we were maybe a thousand feet up at this point. Wesley draped his eyelids over his eyes as he enacted the Trinitarian formula for his last gesture. Sequentially he used his right hand to make the sign of the cross by touching his forehead, stomach, and then shoulder to shoulder in a sweeping motion. In his left hand he gripped the crucifix dangling between his dog tags hanging from his neck. All of the sudden I felt a concussive impact followed by an immediate sensation of heat before my eyes went completely black.

Gasping for air I woke up to find that I was still in the hospital room, I glanced at the pocket watch, the time read three-thirty-three hours. I looked over to see Alondra still sleeping by my side before running my hand through my hair to check for new wounds. I didn't feel any new injuries- I looked down to my legs, all of me was still there. The dream felt so damn much like reality, I needed to know that I was still alive. I pressed against my collar bone which instantly radiated an intense pain confirming my existence. The pain felt just as vividly as I'd felt Wesley's pain in the dream. I tried to collect my thoughts but it was increasingly difficult with all of Dwight's memories and now Wesley's too taking up permanent residence in my head. Usually after a dream I could only recount specific details but this- this was different. I still knew everything. I looked back down at the pocket watch to re-examine the thing. It's convex crystal face refracted the hospital room's thin dim emergency light that always stayed on and caught the reflection of the red blinking lights on the medical equipment behind me as I outstretched my hand holding the watch parallel to the walls. I flipped the watch over to see the faint etching of some sort of writing on its base metal back but was unable to make out any of the words. The entire watch was decently tarnished to a point that you could tell it had been used for a long time yet it still ran flawlessly. I wanted to know how it was still working after all of this time; I affixed it in both my palms as I gave a pressurized counter-clockwise twist. Immediately, it's metal back faintly gave way to my movement directly loosening the metal thread's grip which allowed me to unscrew it and reveal it's elegant mechanized skeleton. I was immediately transfixed with the sheer beauty of the watch's movement- it's five gears all eloquently caught one another's teeth in unison. This propelled a main silver cog fixed with weighted gold pins that cycled it in one-hundred and eighty degree twists revolving both clockwise and counterclockwise. In turn, this propelled three other glimmering gold wheels to slowly impel themselves off of the seemingly infinitely repeating motion. Amidst the middle of the mechanical symphony sat a single red jewel that appeared to glow with the luminescence of a burning ember in the end of a cigarette. With the exception of the three gold cogs, everything else was a slick reflective silver- it was so clean that it looked like some sort of alien medical instrument. On the bottom left of the watch's movement the words,

'HAMILTON WATCH CO.

U.S.A'

were transcribed in a circular arching black gothic font. This trailed another inscription that was in the same font but placed directly on the bottom of the watch's movement parallel to it's crown which read,

'4992B

22

Jewels'

with another red gem placed just a few centimeters in front of the word *Jewels'*. The last thing that stole my attention was a series of numbers and letters depicted deep inside the bowels of the mechanisms, *'4C616333'* again in the same haunting font. My soul was mesmerized by the presence- the power- that seemed to radiate from this omnipresent deity of time. It felt like it was an extension of my body. Screwing the base metal back of the watch back together, the elegant skeleton of this obviously inanimate creature was emblazoned into my mind. I could see it vividly inside my consciousness even when my eyes were plastered shut. My eyelashes intertwined one another as if they were long lost lovers holding hands as the golden highlighted silver movement of the watch's gears cycled perpetually behind my darkened vision. The rhythmic pulsing of my watch's white sweeping second hand clacked away, subtly reverberating through my clutched palm in a manner that mimicked my own gently pounding heart. The metronome melody submersed my entire body in a state of expansive bliss that could not be rivaled- not even by the morphine drip seeping into my circulatory system intravenously in the creak of my left arm. Without even looking, my hands worked in sync to wind the silver peaking crown of the watch once more- even though my eyes remained closed I could feel my pupils swell to the size of pennies. My olfactory senses were suddenly entrenched with an unmistakable scent of wet humid copper that I instinctively knew was blood- just as I slipped out of consciousness.

Propellers ripped violently at a grassy field which was illuminated only by a yellow tinged glow of a fire that cut through the darkness of the night. The ravenous flames were emanating from the remnants of a plane to which the wheezing propellers were once securely affixed. I observed the scene from a distance of approximately 100 yards away through the eyes of someone else. I knew that I was in the middle of an expansive field in Germany, somewhere north of Hamburg. Once again the universe had somehow granted me with an omnipresence that allowed me to immediately comprehend I was witnessing reality from the filter of another person's view. That's exactly how I had the wherewithal to know that my name was Terrance. I was the gunner of that downed B-17, it was most likely the plane that I had just parachuted out of a few minutes earlier with Darrell and Will. Terrance was still riding high on the wave of adrenaline he got from the whole situation that just transpired. Even so, he balled up his parachute and proned out on his stomach amongst the grass to maintain a lower profile as he carefully observed the wreckage of their plane. He looked around the field for any signs of the rest of the crew, but to no avail. He didn't know that Wesley and JR were dead from the crash, nor did he know where Darrell and Will were. The blare of German bomb raid sirens echoed throughout the air, it was only interrupted by the crackling of the fire bellowing from the wreck. I could feel the heat from the flames on Terrance's face even though we were a considerable distance away. Terrance was desperate to link up with a member of his crew before attempting to make his way towards the Danish border. In a whisper pitch he yelled out,

"Will... Darrell... Darrell... JR... Wesley!" fishing for a response. Hanging on the few brief moments to hear something back before calling out again in the same tone,

"Anyone there... ?"

Again, his words fell upon deaf ears- no response. He knew that it was only a matter of time before the Germans sent a patrol out to the crash site- he also assumed that there would be multiple German patrols looking for any survivors. Even so, Terrance was inclined to stay put for at least a little while before moving on. Acting as his inner voice I urged him,

"Go, the Germans are coming! Wesley and JR are dead, it's impossible to know where Will and Darrell are. Maybe we can meet up with them later. The fact that we're near the crash is improbable- finding anyone else from our crew is damn near impossible!"

Terrance's free will instantly rejected my input as his inner voice, he thought to himself,

"I have to get to the plane to see if anyone went down with it. There's no way Wesley or JR are dead- if they're still there I NEED to help them!"

Again I pleaded with him,

"*They're dead- you will be too if you don't make it to the border. Go- go now.*"

Once again he completely disregarded his inner voice, he was strategizing the best way to get to the crash site. He peered over his left and right shoulder before his eyes made their way back to the flames. He deduced that he was safe enough to run straight to the emblazoned wreckage. Understanding his quick conclusion I interjected,

"*Do not go towards the crash site. The fuel can explode, we will die. The Nazis are coming. Run away, far away.*"

That's when I realized the totality of free will, a strong individual had the ability to completely disregard thoughts of doubt, even their own. It is difficult to comprehend such a blatant disregard for one's own life especially when the preservation of our own lives is at the forefront of our animalistic interests. From his thoughts I could tell that he too was plagued by the all too familiar instinct of self preservation, yet there was something inside of him that was able to push that to the side. Briefly I grappled inside my own mind with what exactly that something was- courage? Or maybe it was a false sense of invincibility from the adrenaline? Could it be cockiness, faith, or a lack of understanding in consequences? What if I had told Wesley to take the parachute and leave one of his crew mates to suffer the same grim fate he had? Would he have done it? Would he have fought off thoughts of cowardice in the same manner as Terrence? Were my thoughts that of a coward- was I a coward?

What if...

My intellectual inaction was immediately interrupted by Terrence's direct action, he sprang to his feet and began sprinting towards the wreckage. Our vision shook violently from side to side with each step as our foot made a brief contact with the earth before propelling each of our legs up and forward so quickly that at any one point in time only one of our legs had contact with the ground. The crash site got bigger and bigger in our view as we became closer- with equal intensity, it got much hotter. The flames burned white against the dark contrast of the night, the rods of our eyes were not able to adjust so I could no longer see anything beyond the fire. The thick grey smoke choked out what was left of our view as we approached closer to what was once our plane. Now it was a mangled heap of metal, fuel, and human remains. The smoke did not smell like a campfire, it had a distinct metallic scent that was vaguely outlined by the familiar smell of meat cooking on a charcoal grill- which was confusing to our senses. The toxic metallic smell along with the sight of the mangled plane registered instantly with our consciousness conclusion that the plane was indeed the wreckage. That smell of barbecued meat was still unplaced until it was accented with the unforgettable aroma of burning hair- that's when we saw it. Thrown some fifteen feet from the body of the plane was Wesley's remains. What was left of his head was cocked violently to the right so that his nose was unnaturally parallel with the ground. Half of his body was silently cooking from the emboldened flames that were truly indifferent as to what they consumed. Judging by the apparent charred skeletal remains of his lower torso and lack of movement, it was all too clear that he was dead. Even so, it didn't fully register inside Terrance's mind that Wesley was undoubtedly gone- death was not a reality that he could accept for his brother in arms. Terrance bewilderedly cried out, "Wesley!" as he approached closer to his gruesome remains. The heat was unbearable but Terrance still was able to grab ahold of Wesley's arm in an attempt to pull him to safety. I could feel the unnatural radiant heat emitting from Wesley's forearm and into Terrance's clenched hands as he quickly dragged away his limp weight. After a dozen or so feet, Terrance stopped abruptly, taking off his jacket to fan out the flames still consuming the body. Then he dragged the smoking remains to a tree that was approximately fifty feet away from the fire before attempting to prop up his torso against the trunk for support.

Terrance exclaimed, "Oh God- oh God! What did they do to you? Oh God!"

Wesley's head drooped from his neck making a ghastly wound visible. We both fought feelings of nausea and disbelief off as we patted his jacket pockets looking for the letter to his family that Terrance knew he kept. Typically they all kept their goodbye letters in their right left front breast pocket- but that portion of the jacket was fused to the corpse's skin. He continued the frantic search but to no avail; there was nothing salvageable left. We just wanted to give Wesley the dignity that he deserved and do right by his family if we were ever to make it back home. Defeated, Terrance buried his head amongst the tall grass until he felt the dirt of the earth imprint itself on his forehead. In an attempt to prevent himself from screaming, he clawed at the random flowers and blades of grass as he clenched fistfulls of it all in his now white knuckles. I attempted to console Terrance, *"It will be okay. He's okay now. No more pain, no more worry, no more of anything. Just peace. For him, the war is over. He did not die in vain."*

As Terrance looked up from the ground, the glint of something shimmering in the light of the moon caught his eye. He crawled ten feet towards the glare, when he got there, he knew immediately what the object was- it was Wesley's pocket watch. He picked it up without me prompting him, he knew exactly what it was and he quickly deduced that it must have fallen out of Wesley's pocket as he was dragging him. The way that the watch's front facing crystal refracted the moonlight looked exactly how the watch glimmered when it caught the fluorescent light from my hospital room. I knew that this was not the first time that Terrance had been in possession of the watch because I had some of his memories ingrained in my mind but they were all extremely blurry. I couldn't make sense of them until this exact moment when he once again had the watch, all of his memories became clear. I did my best to ignore them by implicitly just accepting them in my own mind because I knew that time was not on our side. The German sirens were still being carried through the brisk evening air, I knew that we needed to go. Terrance hastily stashed the watch in his right breast coat pocket before surveying the field to make his escape. Suddenly in the distance he could hear German voices clamoring in an angry tone but could not decipher any of their foreign words! I told Terrance, "*Run!*" this time he did not object. He began to sprint towards the north, or at least what he thought was north. That's exactly when I noticed a beam of light sweep in front of him, the light's path was interrupted briefly when it was shined on his back- this produced a thirty foot shadow of Terrance that was unmistakable. We both instantly knew that the Germans had spotted us! We heard an angry shout, "Da ist er! Hör auf Amerikaner!" that instantly confirmed our fears! The voice was followed by the vicious barking of what had to have been at least three fully grown German Shepherds. From the desperate pitch of their barks I could tell that they were hungry for blood and we were their first meal of the week. I knew that we couldn't outrun the German Shepherds but I also knew that we had no other option left but to try! If he was caught I knew that the fate he would suffer would be one worse than death. I told him, "*Don't let them take you alive.*" , advice I think he quickly absorbed. The barking from the dogs grew louder as they drew closer before one of the dogs suddenly leaped up and affixed his jaws on Terrance's left tricep. The shooting pain expanded through all of his nerve endings starting in his arm and ending at his throbbing heart! The momentum of the dog's bite paired with the crippling pain quickly took Terrance to the ground! In an instant the other two dogs were on top of him taking random bites all along his body! The dog's teeth felt like fire as they relentlessly ripped through his flesh! He yelled out in pain as I thought to him

"Shoot them!"

He reached down to his right side in an attempt to remove his Colt 1911 from his leather holster! After a brief struggle with the holsters top button, he was able to remove the gun and get off a shot! The explosion of the bullet initiated an incessant ringing in our ears, the bullet itself was lodged between the ribs of one of the dogs; the dog let out a sick feeble cry before retreating. The other dogs followed suit, being dispersed by the gunshot. Everything happened so damned fast- when he looked up we saw four German soldiers with submachine guns pointed straight at us before being blinded by the spotlight affixed to the military vehicle they had been in! The Germans yelled something out that was inaudible but clearly angry, before I could even think, Terrance raised his 1911 and shot at the direction of the light! Immediately following his first two shots, I felt the hot lead from the German's bullets begin to relentlessly slice through Terrance's midsection before the light fled from my vision and I no longer felt anything at all.

Resisting Reality

When I regained consciousness I was still in the hospital room, everything was the same as it had been before I fell asleep with the exception of the time, it was now mid morning. The sun gently poked through the slit of the blue drapes covering the lone window emitting a dim yellow glow against the walls. I was happy to be alive but other than that, I was confused. I attributed my strange dreams to the morphine I was still on. My entire existence felt fake, almost as if I was in the deep fog of a nightmare. The drugs dulled my overall feeling of existence and mental alertness so that my entire being was in a sheer state of pure indifference. I wanted to get out of the hospital as quickly as possible but I wasn't necessarily sure why. Laying there I decided that I would quit my job at the dealership, I was done with that shit. I didn't have a back up plan but I didn't really care either. I felt that everything would somehow find a way to work itself out. Having a near death experience truly has a way of reshaping your life's perspective. My life's priorities were Alondra, my health, and our happiness- in that order. In front of all of that though was the watch, it lived rent free inside of my mind; it was in an entire category of it's own league in terms of what mattered to me. It was almost as if I needed to have it; the circumstances that joined our paths were more than coincidental, to me it was fate. I began to regard it as my good luck charm in a way, I knew that I could rely on it as much as it could rely on me. It was a symbiotic relationship- or at least it was to me. I did think it was odd that everyone who had been in possession of the watch had died, with the exception of me. I was not sure if it was dangerous or docile; I figured only time would tell. All I really knew was how I felt when it was with me - I was emboldened beyond humanly constraints. I felt a manufactured pleasure that exceeded any other type of worldly feeling I'd ever experienced. It was sheer ecstasy; I felt like there was nothing in the world that could hold me back- I felt powerful. For the first time in my life I felt that my future was mine to shape. I no longer had to have my life dictated to me through bullshit expected ideations pressed upon me by society.

Only I would dictate my future- I would no longer be enthralled by a civilization of maniacs dedicated to the praise of their God: The Almighty Dollar. That being said, another reason I needed out of the hospital was because I knew damned well I couldn't afford to be there. As if on cue with my thoughts, the nurse knocked on my slightly ajar door before entering, "How are we doing?" she said.

I said, "Not too bad- do you by chance know when I'll be able to get out of here?"

She said, "Hopefully soon, you had a pretty severe concussion so we just wanted to monitor you throughout the night and make sure you didn't fall asleep. As far as your collar bone, we are going to take off those straps and set you up with a cast before you go home."

Confused, I asked, "But... I was asleep?"

She said, "No, I've been in every fifteen minutes- you haven't slept. That's probably why you're so tired."

She shined a flashlight in my eyes as she said, "Look up- look down... it looks like your concussion is gone now. Don't worry, confusion is very common, especially with that severe of head trauma. But don't worry, we did CT scans of your head and you have no brain damage. Everything is working as it should be- you're very lucky."

I said, "I am definitely lucky... I could have swore that I was asleep..."

She said, "That's the confusion mixed with the morphine most likely. Soon Dr. Reyes will be in for a final evaluation and then we should be able to get you out of here. Do you have any questions?"

I had a million questions but didn't want her to think that I was crazy.

I said, "Nope, thank you- I appreciate it."

I kept a cheesy smile posted between my thin dry lips until she exited the room. Alondra was still asleep so I couldn't ask her to reaffirm what had gone on throughout the night. Had I really not slept? Had she really been in the room every fifteen minutes? If so, I had no recollection of it at all. Finally, I head a yawn from Alondra, I looked over to see that her eyes were now cracked open halfway.

I said, "Good morning baby! How'd you sleep?"

She said, "Good morning- okay. How are you feeling?"

I said, "I'm not sure. I think I'm okay... was I asleep last night?"

She said, "I'm not sure, I was out. I actually slept pretty good."

I didn't want to let on that something felt very wrong because I didn't want to freak her out.

I said, "That's good. We should be able to get out of here

soon. The nurse said that after the doctor comes in and has one last look at me that I can be checked out."

She said, "That's great baby! So everything is okay?"

I said, "That's what they're saying- no brain damage, my concussion is gone, and I just have a broken collar bone. So all things considered, I'm pretty lucky!"

"That's great!" She exclaimed

Outwardly I echoed her excitement but inside I knew that something was different. I was a different man than I was yesterday, that's for certain.

Waiting on the doctor was tedious to say the least, I understand that they have a lot of other patients but damn! It took forever for Dr. Reyes to come in and give his blessing for me to be able to get out of there. The thing that always baffled me the most was that doctors spent maybe thirty seconds to a minute, if even that, with each patient unless they were actually doing surgery or something like that. Even so, it took hours just to see a doctor that was going around doing his regular 'patient rounds'. It's something that's always perplexed me because the time spent with each patient just doesn't add up. There are patients and their families literally left in limbo for hours just to hear a few official words from the doctor- it's always just struck me as strange. Doctors wield so much power in every aspect, they literally can manipulate life and death. I've always theorized about the moral implications of medical practices- they kill a lot of people. They also save a lot of people; but at the same time they're manipulating human nature- life itself. What gives a human being the right to possess the power of dictating life and death? None of us are any better than anyone else, so how could someone be literally granted a God status? In the caverns of my mind I've also explored the possibility that maybe they're not altering fate at all, maybe fate is destined to run its course perpetually throughout time regardless of the input of others. What if others' actions and inputs into the world and our lives had no real impact on destinies or our fates? Instead, what if people's actions just delayed the inevitable from happening or in some cases sped the inevitable up? Either way though, there's no escaping the inevitable- so, did the tragic or happy details that compose our lives between the time we're thrust onto the Earth in flesh and blood and then absorbed back into the very soil from which we came ever even matter at all? All of our actions cause equal and opposite reactions in the form of consequences that are both negative or positive depending upon what our perception is. With our existences being so inconsequential in the grand scheme of things, did our actions and consequences even have any ramifications at all? In a weird way I felt that all of the world was connected in some sort of unspoken symbiosis that omnipresently dictated life in an unbiased, uncaring manner. Nothing we ever could do would ever prevent our planet from continuing it's unrelenting rotation in space amongst a galaxy of other planets as plentiful as grains of sand in the sea. We are nothing more than inconsequential minute blips in time; the only thing that makes us feel as if that's not true is the fact that we humans possess a cognitive consciousness which allows us to have thoughts about our thoughts and then even develop thoughts of those thoughts. Our egos are designed by nature to elevate our own stature in the world because it's our best tool at self preservation. It's nothing more, nothing less- just like us. In that aspect, we are no different from any other living organism. For example, viruses have the same animalistic goals as humans- to stay alive and reproduce. That's all we do too, the only difference is that we have an ego and consciousness. All of these thoughts of mine made me at peace with the fact that I was dictating thoughts to other people in the dreams I was having- sure it impacted them but could it impact anything else? I mean, even if it did- would it matter? At this point though, I didn't know if the dreams were dreams at all. If I wasn't asleep and these were recollectable memories burned into my mind then I had to have been there, right? These 'dreams' had to have actually happened; they had to have been reality. To me, they were my reality- I can still smell the smoke, I can still feel the pain, the fear- everything. If I experienced something which was to me, reality- then it had to be, right? Who could dispute something that I knew to be true through actually living it?

I looked at my watch to see that three hours had elapsed since the time I had spoken with the nurse before hearing a brief half hearted permissive knocking on my hospital room' slightly ajar door. Briskly entering my room was a six foot tall man draped in grey scrubs exuding a confidence that only a doctor has. He wasted no time as he grabbed for a box of blue non-latex medical gloves hanging from the wall. He began to put them on while saying, "I'm Dr. Reyes, I wish we could have met under different circumstances but it's good to meet you. How are you feeling?"

I said, "It's good to meet you too- I've been better but I'm okay."

He said, "That's understandable, you had quite the concussion- I'm just going to check your eyes."

He approached my bed side and a small pen light emerged from his pocket and into his hand.

"Okay." I said

He shined the light in my face as he said, "Look up... Look down... Left... Now right... Perfect, thank you. Everything looks normal; your brain scans all indicate normal brain activity and I think you're good to go. I'm just going to have a look at your collar bone, then we will get you set up with a new sling and you will be on your way."

I said, "That sounds good to me- thank you Dr."

As he pulled back my hospital gown from my shoulder he said, "Ahh, very good- clean break. Sometimes these bones get shattered and protrude out from the chest cavity and cause all sorts of issues. I looked at your x-rays and seeing the bruising now, it's clear that you're good to go. I'll sign your discharge papers, the nurse will get you wrapped up and you will be out of here. Do you have any questions for me?"

I said, "No sir- thank you very much, I appreciate it."

He noticed the glare of my pocket watch, looking down at it as it caught his eye.

He said, "Hey, that's a Hamilton 4992B- those are beautiful watches. The watch that won the war, as my great grandfather used to say. He used to have one just like that one!"

My inner voice told me that his great grandfather was Darrell.

I asked, "Was your great grandfather's name Darrell?"

Dr. Reyes cocked his head slightly to the side as a cheeky smile overtook his lips before they curled out when he said, "It was- how'd you know that?"

I said, "Lucky guess."

"Hmm, interesting- you should buy a lottery ticket when you get out of here. You seem to be on a roll."

I looked over to Alondra and said, "I've already won."

Dr. Reyes smiled before pointing his index finger at me and saying, "Smart man! You guys take care!"

Then he left the room as quickly as he had entered. Alondra grabbed my hand and said, "I love you."

I looked into her beautiful greenish hazel eyes before telling her the same, "I love you too baby.".

Alondra and I waited a bit longer in silence with the exception of MASH playing on the hospital TV, but that was hardly even audible. The nurse came in one last time, I signed some paperwork and she gave me instructions to pick up a pain medication before I was fully discharged. Once the nurse left the room, I got dressed and meandered out of the hospital, holding onto Alondra as my guide. When we finally breached the inordinately glass sliding doors, they opened automatically to reveal the afternoon to us. I inhaled a deep breath of downtown Denver's caustic air as I let the warmth of the sun overcome me. With my eyes closed, proprioception guided my face towards the burning star- even a million miles away it emitted the comforting warmth of life and was so bright that it made the inside of my eyelids appear red. I was happy to be alive- it's the little things that you have to stop and take a moment to appreciate. It really can help put your life into perspective and help form some sort of meaning out of it all- if even just for a moment. As Alondra and I walked hand in hand toward her car I said, "I never want to be in a damned hospital again!"

She said, "I'll be sure to kill you in your sleep then."

We both laughed as I feebly attempted to lodge myself into the passenger seat- with the sling I had to maneuver myself just right so that I could fit. Since this was my first go at it, I knew it would take some time to get used to. Since we were already out, we picked up my new prescription from the pharmacy before heading home. I'm glad we did too, because by the time we were back at the apartment, I could already feel the pain from my collar bone and head begin to slowly evolve. It transitioned from dull lingering uncomfort to a nerve rattling throbbing, aching pain that was much more intense. I ripped open the bag containing the orange tinged plastic child proof pill bottle before reading the name out loud, "Oxycodone, thirty milligrams. Take one pill every twelve hours as needed for pain." I wish I would have paid more attention to the nurse or even the pharmacist at this point. I don't know if I could take it yet or not, I yelled out to Alondra who was in our bedroom, "Baby- do you think I should take this pill now or wait awhile? I'm starting to hurt worse."

She yelled back, "Just wait awhile, you probably still have

stuff in your system from the hospital. Are you going to take a shower? You probably should."

I hollered back, "Yeah, I just don't know how with this damned sling. I'll have to wear half a trash bag or something."

She started running the shower for me, I put the pills back on the kitchen counter and went to the bathroom to undress. I knew I still had the watch with me, it was in my front left pants pocket. I partly didn't want to shower because I didn't want to be without it, even if just for a few moments- it was odd. I walked into the bedroom and set the watch delicately on my nightstand before preparing myself for the shower, which now was going to be quite the process. Instantly I felt very strange, I could feel the clawing of anger at the base of my head and all I could think about was the watch. I needed it with me, I wanted it with me. I had to have Alondra stop the waterproofing process of enclosing ¾ of my torso in a bag so that I could go back to the watch. Every ounce of my being needed it; I took a few steps back into our room and picked up the watch. Immediately my feelings of anger melted away, I felt like I was back to normal. Then I gave the crown of the watch a few winding turns, that's when I felt it again- that bliss, that sheer ecstasy. My pain even dulled it was utterly amazing- I never wanted the feeling to end. I never wanted to be without the watch. Alondra yelled out to me,

"What are you doing? Come on, let's get this done."

I said, "I'm coming, I thought I heard my phone. I thought it was the hospital."

I gazed into the crystal of the watch transfixed by the sweeping second hand ticking away without a care in the world before I begrudgingly set it back on my nightstand. It must have been a very odd sight to see from an observer's eye, a fully grown naked man draped in a trash bag staring at a pocket watch. I laughed at the thought and as I entered the bathroom I said, "I think I'm still high as hell. I feel really weird."

Alondra said, "It's possible- I don't know the half-life of morphine but it's got to be a while."

I raised my eyebrows and shook my head as if I were trying to sober up before saying, "Yeah, damn."

Those same feelings of anger began to overcome me, the longer I was away from the watch, the worse I felt. Alondra finished bagging me up and I hopped into the shower- that's when I got even worse. Instantly I felt nauseous and my head began to pound with a ferociousness that I've never experienced. The water was lukewarm but I began to shake, almost as if I was going through a withdrawal. I half heartedly attempted to lather my thick black hair with shampoo- I could feel small sharp shards of glass or other debris from the accident still entangled so I proceeded with caution. In search of some relief from my rapidly deteriorating state I cried out to myself, "Shit! This sucks!"

The profanity helped get me through rinsing the remaining shampoo from my now heavy head. I cut the shower as short as I could so that I could get back to the watch and hopefully feel better. I left the water running for Alondra as I exited the stained tub-shower in a haste. I quickly dried off before snatching my watch from the nightstand and settling into bed. This time, relief wasn't instantaneous- instead it took a few moments to feel better even though I had the watch clutched in my palm. It was as if the watch was giving me a warning to not go without it again- like it was being spiteful even though it knew it held complete power over me. Alondra came into the bedroom, our eyes locked and she exclaimed, "Damn! Your eyes are as bloodshot as hell! Are you alright baby?"

Unsure of my state, I said, "I don't know, I was feeling even worse in the shower. Now that I'm laying down I feel a bit better. Can you grab me some water and one of those pain pills please- I think I need it.

"Sure" she said as she went to retrieve my legal drugs. Seeking a quick fix to my ailments, I began winding the watch- instantly my entire body warmed. I was overcome by the now familiar feelings of bliss- however it didn't feel as good as it had the first time. That first time... was an inexpressible high, the likes of which are just incomprehensible. Now it was as if I was chasing that euphoric feeling- every ounce of my being yearned for it. Trying to exude an appearance of normalcy, once Alondra came back into our room I outstretched my hand towards her while saying, "Thank you.".

I pressed the pill between my dry cracked lips while I fumbled around with my free hand in search of the water bottle perched on our bed's end table. I gulped the pill down with the water before resigning my ambitions to just laying there in bed.

I could see the inside crook of an elbow covered in a dark black sleeve that ended just an inch or so from a wrist that was holding a Luger pistol. My eyes made their way from the bronze inscribed cufflinks with the letters 'SS' in an embold- ened red and adjusted themselves on the front sight of the Luger as the rear sights became blurred. In a heap in front of the Luger was Terrance, now dead, in a mangled mess- he was almost cut entirely in half. I heard a heinously graveled voice yell out from behind me,

"Erschieße das Yankee-Schwein!"

I understood exactly what the soldier said, I even knew that it was Schutzstaffel Sergeant Fritz Heimlocsh who yelled it. Without hesitation I could feel the quick sloppy jerk of this man's index finger on the trigger- I felt the explosions of the bullets thud in my chest and smelled the gunpowder bury itself in his nose. I was now intertwined in the mind of Schutzstaffel Lance Corporal Karl Walter. He grimly laughed as he pointlessly shot Terrance's dead body, after four shots he called out to the other troops behind him,

"Es muss mehr geben (There must be more)"

Fritz said,

"Suchen Sie mindestens zwei nach etwas Wertvollem, bevor wir die anderen zusammenfassen. (At least two, search him for anything valuable before we round up the others.)"

Then he kneeled down to frisk Terrance's body- his calloused dirty hands found their way to a blood soaked map, a zippo lighter, and then the watch. He stashed the watch and the zippo in his pocket and then held up the map in the light of the searchlight to try to decipher it. I could read the map as easily as I could understand German- Karl however could not read or understand English at all. I was not about to help him either, that's for sure. I was stunned to find myself in the consciousness of a nineteen year old Nazi- SS even, the worst of the worst. Once I came to this realization I expected to be disgusted- I thought that this brainwashed Nazi would be a despicable miserable man with twisted thoughts and possess dreadful details of the war. Karl gave up trying to read the map after turning it upside down and every which way in the light in a last ditch effort. He creased the map in half as he walked towards Fritz, he outstretched it to him and said,

"Here, I can't read it, it's in pig Latin. We will have to bring it back to the camp to the translators. Are we taking the other prisoners alive?"

Even though they were speaking in fast, seemingly angry tones of German, I heard it as English.

Fritz said, "Commandant Gruber's orders are to take them alive unless we meet resistance. Let's find the others."

Karl, Fritz, and two other SS officers all got into their half track military vehicle with Fritz behind the wheel. There was another vehicle accompanying them with another four SS offi- cers occupying that one. Fritz yelled out to the troops, "Keep your eyes peeled." before driving off into the night in search of any other survivors. Karl was sitting in the front passenger seat operating the spotlight. His thoughts were irreverently sporadic about nothing in particular which I found to be odd because they had all just killed a man. I knew that this was not the first life he had taken, he's had many other victims. He however did not consider those that he'd killed to be victims, in his mind they were enemies of the German Reich- he was simply doing his duty to his nation. From his memories, I could tell that he had been a member of the Third Reich's infamous Hitler's Youth group prior to joining the ranks of the Schutzstaffel at sixteen. His deep blue eyes, thick blonde hair and six foot three inch stature definitely paved the road to his admittance into the SS. He honestly felt proud to be part of the wretched murderous group, it gave him and his family a safety that was unparalleled in Germany at that time. He was able to provide food and money to his parents and two younger siblings back home in Berlin. He also considered himself amongst the elite of the Nazi party, this was something that his father Grubitz pressed further into his mind. Grubitz had fought in World War One in the decades prior, which left him with innumerable physical and mental injuries that were beyond repair. The years after the war left Germany destitute; their overinflated currency was worthless, there were no jobs, no pride, and even no humanity left in the German state. They were a deeply fractured nation, the victors of the war further ensured this to teach Germany a lesson. The German people themselves were beyond a desperate state- they were ashamed to exist, the poverty wrought throughout the nation made the sheer act of existing next to impossible. Food was as scarce as the job prospects were; Karl grew up in a shack of a dwelling in the outskirts of South Berlin. Most of his child-hood nights were spent sleeping on a cold creaky wooden floor in a one room flat that the whole family shared. The persistent water leaks from its derelict roof were as frequent an occurrence as the incessant rumblings of his malnourished stomach. When Grubitz wasn't drinking away his pain at sorrow in the beer halls he was raising hell in that one room flat they all shared. He would beat his wife Helga, Karl, his younger brother Hans, and even his younger sister Anna with a ferociousness that almost left Karl's mother Helga dead on multiple occasions. In this aspect though, Karl was not alone, in every other flat in their building each separate family lived out essentially the same hellish reality day in and day out. It was no way to live- seemingly any hope in the souls of the German people died after the war. It was as if everyone carried about their lives in an intoxicated stooper, violently fueled even further from the treacheries they all had lived in the war. To survive, they needed someone other than themselves that they could blame. This is exactly why they would frequently beat their families and kill one another, there were no prospects of life- until the National Socialist German Workers' Party emerged. Over the nineteen-twenties and thirties this new political party started to slowly grow in numbers and prevalence in Germany. The party brought nationwide attention with their 'Beer Hall Putsch' spearheaded by their new overzealous self proclaimed leader, Adolf Hitler. This man pontificated to the lost souls of Germany throughout countless beer halls and various venues reigniting pride in their nation and ultimately providing the German people with a sense of hope. After the Beer Hall Putsch he was briefly imprisoned, during his tenure in jail his prevalence grew and he wrote a book detailing his vision as to how to save Germany. Upon his release his book became a bestseller in Germany which helped propel him and the National Socialist German Workers' Party to power. On January thirtieth, nineteen thirty-three Hitler was appointed as Chancellor by President Paul von Hindenburg. The National Socialist German

Workers' Party grew from a few hundred members to over hundreds of thousands of members. As Chancellor, Hitler grew his influence in the party and secured it using his 'Sturmabteilung' Storm Troopers (SA)- known as Brownshirts and the Schutzstaffel (SS), which were known as Blackshirts militiamen. Initially these militias were used to give jobs to countless German men who had been out of work for years- now they once again could provide for their families. Slowly their sense of national pride, dignity, and standard of living were all increasing. This is most likely why they all started to turn a blind eye to the antisemetic racist rhetoric that they were all becoming entrenched in through fervently effective but disgusting propaganda. Little did they know that this was just the beginning of Hitler's twisted vison of death, destruction, and genocide. In March of nineteen thirty-three an act was passed in parliament expanding Hitler's power far beyond the constraints of parliament. He created jobs through revamping the nation's civilian infrastructure, military, and began a facade campaign reinvigorating German. He truly exploited the German people via temporarily giving them and telling them exactly what they wanted - it worked so well that he was soon to be revered by many brainwashed people as a deity. All the while he was securing his power via the SA, SS, and now the entire German military turning the nation into a fearful antisemetic police state, of which he had complete and total power. Germany had sanctions imposed as to their ability to grow their military personnel and assets, however the world chose ignorantly not to enforce them. Grubitz was a member of the SA, his drinking and abuse all but ended once he again found meaning though a false mission. This was the case for millions of others as well. Grubitz enrolled Karl in the Hitler's youth program just before it became a mandatory requirement for all children. It's no excuse, but Karl was in effect nothing more than a product of his environment. The scariest part about it all was that Karl felt in his heart that he was as right-eous as I knew he was wrong- I could tell. Righteousness is amongst the most fatal diseases that anyone has ever suffered from- countless horrors have been committed all under the glorious guise of 'righteousness'. I knew the horrors that Karl did not- I knew about the genocide occurring on the camps, I was more than surprised when I realized that he had no idea. To him, the Jewish people were an enemy of the state who were all responsible for Germany losing the First World War- this was ingrained into him from the relentless Nazi propaganda that he was constantly subject to. He thought that the Jewish people were responsible for how Germany was after the war- as thus they were all vicariously liable for the countless beatings he watched his family endure. All the bruises and the countless broken bones they suffered from at the hands of his father were really from the aforementioned race- at least in his mind. While this was beyond a case of faulty logic and the furthest thing from the truth, he accepted it as gospel, it was his truth. How could you ever change someone's false truth? Hitler effectively manipulated the perception of a nation to perpetuate his sick agenda.

Karl's SS unit never found any other survivors from the crash, nor did I learn their fate, other than what I previously disclosed through our memories. After they stopped their search for survivors they headed back to "Camp Two" where they were all stationed. Camp Two was a prisoner of war camp for the Allies- it was a wretched, godforsaken barbed wire enclosure that consisted of forty-three shacks, where all the allied prisoners were kept. Camp Two was not unique by any means, there were dozens of these camps but their existence was known to the Allies so these camps were ruled differently from the concentration camps. The fact that the Allied forces knew of these camps existence was a primary factor for why genocide didn't occur there. Karl had only been exposed to these prisoner of war camps that he had been stationed in, he had no idea about the concentration camps. Everything in the Nazi regime was kept on a very 'need to know' basis which only perpetuated Karl's sense of importance. Karl's Nazi entourage proceeded to the first security checkpoint of Camp Two, which consisted of a road blockade adjacent to a small guard shack which was manned by four other Nazis. I thought it was interesting that they all stopped at this checkpoint and took the time to show the guards each of their papers that they requested even though they were in full uniform. From Karl's thoughts I could tell that this was always standard procedure, it was as if they didn't even trust one another. This was repeated at another two checkpoints that were both very similar to the first one- then they proceeded into the camp. The camp itself was essentially a small city that had an infirmary, mess hall, recreation field, and guard quarters. The troupe of Nazis parked their vehicles before convening briefly in an Officer's tent to debrief the events of that night's patrol. Fritz tasked Hans, a junior SS Officer, with writing the report of the night's happenings before splitting off to their respective posts. Karl had been up already for twenty-four hours yet I could tell that he wasn't the least bit tired. He walked from the Officer's quarters of the camp through the rows of shanties all while being extremely vigilant of anything that may be out of place. He intricately observed each shanty as he walked past them, but the shacks were in two parallel lines both to his left and right so that he was walking directly in the middle of them. His head would ratchet from left to right so intensely as he passed them that it was very odd- his vision was in effect starting to make me feel nauseated. I told him,

"Relax- all the prisoners are asleep, it's three in the morning."

in an attempt to normalize his behavior but it had absolutely no effect at all. It was almost as if he disregarded his consciousness thoughts and had only two driving thoughts that were implanted in his head: shoot any prisoners outside of their bunks and get to the infirmary. The infirmary was at the very end of the camp, it was positioned twenty five yards past the lines of shanties but directly in the middle of them and only about ten yards from the barbed wire fence that enclosed the entire camp. As soon Karl entered the infirmary he made his way directly to the doctor and said,

"Can you give me more Pervitin?"

Dr. Frueger responded, "Yes- don't tell the others I gave it to you though, our supplies are dwindling."

Karl said, "I won't- I'll just take a bottle of twenty-five for now. That should hold me over for the next week, we have all been doing double duty with all of the planes we've been shooting down. We have to go to each crash site and search for survivors, it's been a real nightmare. Some of these bastards are getting away, it's unacceptable."

Dr. Frueger said, "The Fuhrer would be proud, one way or another they will all be found. There's nowhere for them to go, making it to the border without passing one of our check-points is impossible."

Karl agreeingly said, "I know- but I prefer to get them first. Well, I'll be here until five in the morning. Then I'll be relieved to wake buildings Thirty-Nine through Forty-Four for roll call and breakfast. Let me know if you need anything, I'll be upfront."

Dr. Frueger said, "Sounds good- thank you."

They both gave each other a Nazi salute with a click of their heels and cried out, "Heil Hitler!" before parting ways in opposite directions. I thought this stupid pageantry looked even more ridiculous than it sounded. To me, it demonstrated exactly how brainwashed the Nazis were- even when they were alone, with just the two of them there, they felt this pertinent to do. For them it was as common as shaking hands and Karl didn't even give it a second thought. Before exiting the infirmary Karl took one of the round white Pervitin pills he just received, I was not entirely sure what the pill was. All I could really tell was that he was really craving it, the stuff must have been extremely addicting for him to need it as much as he did. From Karl's thoughts I could tell that he considered Pervitin to essentially be a safe energy booster, like caffeine basically but on steroids. Karl paced back and forth in front of the infirmary for about ten minutes- then I could feel the Pervitin kick in. It was a warming sensation of his entire body, I could literally feel the dopamine receptors in his brain open up like a dam breaking. His thoughts rapidly clamored in his head at a pace that was impossible to follow, so much so that he was essentially no longer in control of his own body. Even so, I could tell that he instantly experienced a deep sense of infallibility outlined by an innate feeling of invincibility. This was followed by a jolt of energy that was so palpable that I could feel his increased level of alertness- which was so focused that he could hear the cracking of the blades of grass off in the distance as rats scurmerred through the fields. Immediately it became clear to me that this 'Pervitin' stuff was some type of powerful amphetamine that was way beyond caffeine. I'd never done drugs before, but from what I've seen and heard I was pretty positive that this was essentially crystal meth! I told Karl,

"You're thirsty, take a drink of water."

in an effort to gauge my influence on him but it had no effect at all. He continued on pacing as his paranoia began to steadily increase about what he was hearing out in the fields. My input on his conscious mind was entirely ineffective, it was almost as if he didn't even hear me. The Pervitin effectively removed any conscious rationality that he may of had. The only thing Karl was concerned with now was when he could take another pill and how he could get more- it was clear that he was addicted to this stuff! It was actually part of his monthly rations but he had been going through the pills too quickly, grossly exceeding the prescribed dosage inscribed on the front label of the brown opaque glass pill bottle that read:

'Take one pill every eight hours for tiredness. Do not take more than three pills in a day.'.

He was popping one or two pills every four hours so it was obvious that he's basically in a constant state of intoxication. This definitely explained why he had not slept in so long or why I can't remember the last time that he had even eaten anything. His sense of time was also severely impacted, it seemed to elapse extremely fast; he reached into his pocket to find his watch but it was gone. Manically frisking the outsides of his trousers, he felt the familiar circular enclosure of a pocket watch- his hand dove into his pocket before reemerging with the unfamiliar watch. Then he remembered that he had taken it from a dead soldier hours ago, this brought a disgusting smile that smugly curled his lips upwards as he briefly admired his new war trophy. The time displayed on the watch was six-hundred hours, but he was skeptical as to its accuracy because it was American made, he assumed. He altered the course of his pacing to head back into the infirmary to verify the time, the clock hanging on the blank white wall to his left also read six o'clock.

"Shit- I'm late!" he said aloud to no one as he ran out of the infirmary towards building Thirty- Nine. It was only a few meters away so he got there quickly. He briefly fumbled with his keys as he attempted to unlock the main doors to the housing unit. The correct key slipped past the jagged teethy opening of the lock's face and turned effortlessly to the right as all of its pins aligned which depressed the main shackle's arm and in effect opened the lock. He left the lock hanging open on the right door before jerking both doors open and screaming,

"Roll call! Get outside now!"

Then he proceeded to unlock buildings Forty through Forty Four before taking his place in front of the amassing prisoners of war in the open space between the buildings. The prisoners stood in rows that were made as artificially uniform as they could while holding up the other dead prisoners in a standing position. All prisoners had to be present for roll call, regardless of whether or not they were dead. This was yet just another demonstration of the Nazis exerting their power over the helpless, it also displayed their viciously bureaucratic practices of recording every finite detail- silvering that I knew would come back to haunt them. The prisoners themselves were all shells of the soldiers that they once were, grossly malnourished skeletons trudging along before being forced to stand in the filth of human excrement and thick mud. All of their blue and white uniforms were stained and tattered- some almost to the point that they barely were wearing a uniform at all... This was a horrid sight to witness. A less senior guard then methodically ran through the roll call name by name, with each prisoner raising their hand in silence as their name was yelled out. Karl said back observing, waiting for any of the prisoners to fall out of line of crumpling under the weight of the dead comrades that they were propping up. I could no longer stand it, I repeated to Karl,

"This is wrong, stop this now! This is wrong, this is wrong... "

My repetition got through to him somehow, his thoughts acknowledged that it was wrong but he pushed back by telling himself,

"This is just business as usual. If I interfere in it, then I too will be shot."

In an instant rebuttal I told him,

"Well it's not right- maybe I deserve to be shot anyway for everything I've done. My personal circumstances are irrelevant

to what I'm doing here now. There are no excuses, there must be something that I can do to help these prisoners."

He acknowledged the thoughts but put them on the back burner of his mind as he continued walking up and down the line of prisoners. I knew that the rent free space in his consciousness that I just acquired was all that I needed- he was beginning to recognize his transgressions by questioning his actions. I knew that planting the seed of questioning things, no matter how subtle, was the beginning of change. As roll call came to a grim close, the prisoners were ordered to do an odd series of stretches all in a haunting synchrony- they were permitted to sing to keep their cadence. Their voices dimly echoed off the shanties as the sound of their voices in unison carried through the camp before dissipating into the woods.

After completing these horrid morning rituals, most of the prisoners broke off into three single file lines to march to the mess building for breakfast. A dozen prisoners stayed behind to collect their dead compatriots left in the mud from roll call. They began to pick each body up, one prisoner would get the legs while another grabbed the body by the arms. They methodically tossed the body's into a cart to be binned away. Shockingly, Karl jumped in by intervening with the prisoners, he looked to the three other SS guards and said,

"This is a waste of time- they take forever every morning doing this. Starting today, it's now your job to dispose of the body's left after roll call."

The SS guards thought Karl was joking, they laughed a hearty belly laugh before one of the men scanned Karl from head to toe before saying,

"If you want to touch the animals, we won't stop you; but we're not touching those pigs."

Karl, exercising his rank over the junior SS Officers yelled at the Officer,

"I'm not asking you, I'm not joking either! How you do it, I don't care- but YOU are going to do it! That's an order! If you don't like it then I'll shoot you myself!"

Karl drew his Luger pistol from his leather holster and affixed the sights between the Officer's eyes.

Karl continued,

"Starting today- starting right now! Get to it!"

The SS Officer walked towards Karl until the Officer's forehead was pressed against the barrel of Karl's Luger before saying,

"You will pay for this- especially if you are becoming partial to the pigs. Commander Fritz will hear about this..."

I told Karl,

"Shoot him! SHOOT HIM!..."

I felt Karl squeeze the trigger with his index finger in a jerking motion- just then, the SS Officer's words were stopped mid sentence. I felt Karls face be splattered with warm blood! The splatter got in Karl's eyes, draping his vision in red for a brief moment. The SS Officer's head seemingly exploded as the bullet entered his skull! His body fell to the mud in a horrid wet thud that was hardly audible over the familiar ringing in Karl's ears! He then pointed the Luger at the other two SS Officer's which put their hands up in shock. These two younger Nazis were not battle hardened like most of the others, so they were essentially docile at the thought of being shot.

Karl yelled at them,

"Don't put him with the pigs. Get to it! Clean this up!"

They did exactly as Karl instructed, he watched them carry the remaining bodies as he dabbed the rest of the blood from his face with a white handkerchief. It took them about thirty minutes to move all of the bodies and get them carted away, the whole time Karl just watched stoically, he was not even concerned about the man he just killed. After they were done,

Karl walked to Commander Fritz's office near the front of the camp- it was only about a five minute stroll. He was getting his story straight the whole walk there- Hans disobeyed a direct order, putting my authority in question, and he was showing preferential treatment towards the prisoners. We both knew that the last part was not true at all, but the guilty often project their 'crimes' or intent on others as a matter of self preservation. I was subtly interfering with his thought process to show him that these prisoners were people- not the evil foreign invaders that the Nazi propaganda machine painted them out to be. Once he started to think of them as people and not 'the enemy' or savages- he felt empathetic towards them. This showed me that beyond all the Pervitin and bias fueled limiting beliefs, that there was still a sense of humanity somewhere inside of him- there was hope.

Once Karl got to Commander Fritz's office building he was met by two other armed SS Officer's guarding the entry door. Karl said,

"I need to speak to Commander Fritz- it's an urgent camp matter."

Amenable by the visits' stated purpose and Karls rank, the two officers stepped aside to allow Karl enter. Once inside he was greeted by a secretary who stood up at attention and did his little goose step salute to Karl before asking if he had an appointment.

Karl said quite plainly,

"No, I don't have an appointment but I need to talk to the Commander about an urgent camp matter. Is he available?"

"Let me check..." the secretary said before making his way to Commander Fritz's office. He knocked three times before cracking the door open just enough to fit his head into the room. I could hear him say something, but I couldn't make it out. After a moment he poked his head back out from the door and said,

"Commander Fritz will see you now."

Karl thanked the secretary before making his way passed him into the commander's office. They both did their little goose step salute rituals, ending the salute by both exclaiming "Heil Hitler!". I made Karl feel embarrassed about doing this, I'm glad that I was able to. Commander Fritz then said,

"Take a seat- what's going on?"

Karl said, "Well we have a problem- some of the guards are becoming partial to the prisoners and are giving them preferential treatment. I've been hearing rumors that the guards have been giving the prisoners more freedom in exchange for cigarettes and chocolate. Today- I witnessed a guard exhibiting this preferential treatment towards the prisoners. He disobeyed a direct order from me and I had to take matters into my own hands and I shot him."

Commander Fritz said,

"Who was the Officer you shot- let me guess- Hans?"

Surprised, Karl said,

"Yes- it was Hans! How did you know?"

Commander Fritz said,

"He's been a trouble maker in F unit, I had my assumptions that it would only be a matter of time. Thank you for keeping order in the camp. Without order, we have nothing."

Karl said,

"Yes sir- I think that to curb the issue of this preferential treatment we need to make it punishable by death for participating in any such conduct with the prisoners. That way the troops know just how serious this is. Anyone caught trading with the prisoners or allowing them extra liberties will be held accountable."

Commander Fritz said,

"That's an excellent idea, consider it done- effective immediately."

Karl knew that by doing this he was in effect signing off on his own death sentence because he was now going to help the prisoners in any way that he could.

Exuding a sense of contentment, Karl said,

"Thank you Commander."

Then he did the dumb goose step salute, uttered the ugly phrase, and pivoted on his left foot which charted his course of direction towards the door and out of the building. As Karl headed to his quarters to rest before his next shift, I inundated his tiring mind with a deluge of thoughts:

"We have to help the prisoners tunnel out of here. We can provide them tools and help loosen security by providing them with even more information about the frequency of patrols. We can notify them before the random barracks searches so that they know well in advance. Eventually this war will be over and the Nazis will lose; being helpful towards the Allied prisoners is our best shot at surviving with a shred of our dignity intact. We can give them part of our rations and even smuggle bread from the mess hall. These prisoners are people- we have to help them. We have to help them...".

I continued to influence him with the truth even once he got to his quarters and began to remove his uniform, the repetitiveness of my thoughts in his mind penetrated deeper than I could ever have imagined. He laid down in his uncomfortably stiff cot as he positioned his now heavy head into his thin down pillow. We stared at the misshapen rotting wood clapboards that adorned the ceiling of his quarters until eventually he drifted into a drug induced state of half lucid, half hallucinating. The wooden clapboard ceiling transformed into a cinematic screen that depicted small fires, smoke, and innumerable dead men- he was again on the front. He could hear the inanimate imagined bullets cut the air above and around him; he felt the concussion of shells explode- his arms maneuvered around violently as if he was shooting his StG 44... I felt my hold of him fade as I began to feel my physical body wretch in a deep nausea.

I woke up in my bed- in my own mind and physical dimension covered in vomit. My entire body felt like I'd been hit by a truck- probably because I really had been. My mouth again began to sweat as my stomach wretched, more stomach acid violently erupted from my mouth. Alondra woke up,

"Oh shit!" she exclaimed before hurrying out of bed in search of a trash can or any sort of vessel to contain my spew. My primary concern was my watch- where was it? I had fallen asleep with it in my hand, I violently frisked the sheets of our bed in search of it! I knew that it would make me feel better, just then I felt it underneath our thin white sheet! I clutched it in my palm, even though it was still wrapped in the sheet. Instantly I felt better- it's as if I was going through with-drawals from it! I untangled it from the sheet and clutched it in my no longer shaking hands- then Alondra got to the bedside with a large red bowl she had fetched from the kitchen. She said,

"Baby are you okay?"

I wiped off the corners of my mouth and said,

"I don't know- I think I am now... that sucked. I'll help you change the sheets, this is disgusting."

I started to get up from the bed as she stopped me by placing her hand on my shoulder- she said,

"Don't get up too fast, just try to relax for a second. Get up slowly."

I heeded to her advice- I took three deep breaths then she helped me up. She continued,

"Did you get any of it on you?"

I shook my head slowly from right to left to indicate my response. I said,

"Maybe I'll just go lay on the couch for a minute... I feel horrible."

She said,

"That's a good idea- do you need help?"

I said, "No- thank you though. I love you."

She responded,

"I love you too."

I slowly walked to the living room couch before remembering that it was probably time to take another pain killer. I gently called out to Alondra,

"On second thought, could you bring me another pain pill and some water?"

"Yes babe- one second." she said.

I settled myself onto the couch, propping my head up a bit with a pillow and laying lengthwise before she came into the room.

"I brought you some applesauce too, so then you don't take it on an empty stomach." she said.

I responded,

"Thank you baby!"

Then I hastily swallowed the horse pill, washing it down with water and then some of the applesauce. I called out again,

"I will change the sheets in a minute babe."

She said,

"Don't worry about it babe, just relax."

"Relax... relax..." I repeated to myself with a false hope of soothing all my physical ailments. I focused my grip on the watch- I didn't want it to fall out of my hand ever again.

EXACTA

I found my vision again entrenched with mindlessly peering up at that damned wooden clapboard ceiling- I was part of Karl's conscious mind once again. Karl had my watch clenched in his hand which was odd to me because he had not previously. Nonetheless, this gave me an even deeper insight into this man's mind. Exhausted, he sat up perched on the corner of his cot as he wiped his eyes. I knew that he was about to reach for his Perviten, he hadn't stopped thinking about it- it engulfed him. I repeated to him haplessly,

"Don't do it- don't take it, you don't need it."

My influence was not even half as powerful as those damned pharmaceutical narcotics; he resigned to his ambitions and took another pill. I thought to him,

"This is killing you- you know that right?"

He rationalized by telling himself that it was harmless and that he needed it. Then he began to put on his gaudy SS uniform before heading out for another twenty-hour day. This had been his routine for so long that he was essentially running on auto-pilot; I still could not believe that he hadn't eaten anything yet. He wasn't even hungry- not even in the slightest, but I saw this as a great opportunity for him to smuggle supplies to the prisoners. I began to repeat to him,

"You're hungry, after roll call you should go to the mess hall and have something to eat. While you're there, you should get bread and spoons for the prisoners."

Karl carried out the disgusting rituals of morning roll call as he had countless times before, except this time I could tell that the tone of his voice was not as incensed. Instead of slamming the barracks doors open and closed, he just did it very firmly- my effect on him was obvious. Throughout roll call I continued repeating the same thoughts in his head to the point that it was impossible to ignore; it was like an itch that he was obligated to scratch at this point. It gnawed at him until he did exactly what I wanted, he scratched the itch by making his way towards the mess hall after roll call. Once his intentions were clear, I stopped my incessant impressions on him because they turned into his own thoughts. The mess hall itself was fairly expansive with an abundance that was absolutely sickening considering the fact that they were the bastards responsible for starving millions. He grabbed his tray and took his place in line amongst a sea of hungry Nazis. He made casual conversation with the officers around him, most of which I could tell that we knew. The only man we didn't know was directly behind us in line, he had an eye patch, no right hand, and only three fingers on his left hand- which was not out of the ordinary, but he was not conversing with the rest of them. This made him stand out in a very bad way among the others, so much so that there was a thickness lingering in the air around the man. The others desperately wanted to confront him to know exactly what his deal was or what he was doing at their camp. The stripes on his uniform made confronting him or even speaking to the man a very bad idea because it was obvious that he was a Colonel. I thought to Karl,

"Introduce yourself to that Colonel."

Karl had no want or desire to do that, especially since he was planning on stealing bread to give to the prisoners. Taking food out of the mess hall for any reason was forbidden, exactly because of that: they didn't want sympathizers giving or trading food to the prisoners. The best way to curtail that was to ensure that no food left the mess hall- violators were reassigned to the front, stripped of rank, or even shot in certain cases. Nonetheless, I persisted to Karl,

"Introduce yourself to that Colonel."

Again he ignored our thoughts and focused his attention to what was on the menu for the day. It was some sort of onion soup with potatoes and a slice of rye bread. The soldier behind the counter was dressed in combat fatigues with a stained kitchen apron over his uniform, it looked absolutely ridiculous. The man heaped a two ladle serving of the dark soup into a bowl, tossed in the rye bread, and handed it to the man in front of Karl. Then Karl got his serving and he made his way towards the officer's seating area near the rear of the building. Once there, Karl took a seat at the empty table, most officers ate before roll call and the majority of the lower ranking soldiers ate after. From behind Karl we heard a voice ask,

"Is this the Officer's seating"

Karl looked back to see the Colonel with the eyepatch, then he sprang up from his seat and said,

"Yes Colonel!"

The Colonel said,

"Good, then I shall join you. At ease, you may take a seat."

He set down his tray and settled into his seat as he asked without even looking up,

"So, Lance Corporal- what is your name?"

Karl introduced himself,

"Lance Corporal Karl Walter."

The Colonel said,

"It's good to meet you Lance Corporal Walter, I am Colonel Claus von Stauffenberg - so why are you eating after roll call with the enlisted men? It's my understanding that Officers like yourself typically eat before?"

Karl said,

"That's correct Colonel, I typically do not eat until late afternoon but today I was hungry earlier."

Colonel Stauffenberg seemingly satisfied responded,

"I understand completely- that too is why I'm here at this time. I'm on a temporary assignment visiting the prisoner of war camps conducting a special report for Hitler.

Karl said,

"That seems like a very important effort, tiring but important."

Colonel Stauffenberg asked,

"Tiring? What do you mean?"

Karl stumbling over his words replied,

"Well... there... well there's just so many of these camps- so it must be tiring to visit them all and have to deal with looking at all the enemy pigs."

Colonel Stauffenberg said,

"That is a good point- I enjoy it but it can be taxing. I prefer to be in Berlin, or even better, on the front... but as you can tell eye am limited by my sight"

Karl picking up on the que that it was a bad joke about the Colonel's lost eye let out a obligatory laugh before saying,

"The enemy is lucky you're here and not on the front- they would all be slaughtered."

Colonel Stauffenberg laughed before he responded,

"Thank you Lance Corporal for your flattery."

Then the two ate silently, Karl felt uncomfortable being in the presence of a Colonel, especially knowing about the transgressions he was about to commit. Now Karl had to figure out how he could smuggle out the bread and the cutlery with the Colonel still there. His initial plan was to do a random inspection of the kitchen, because of his rank, it would not even be questioned. Now however he was concerned that the Colonel would see him conduct the fake inspection or even walk in on him while he was carrying it out. There was a deluge of potential issues that could arise, all of which for me, seemed like far removed ramifications. I figured that if Karl was caught, then it would just be collateral damage so I thought to him,

"Go with the original plan. Get up, take your tray, do your little Nazi salute thing and do the kitchen inspection."

Karl did exactly that, the Colonel did not seem surprised or suspicious of it at all- he wanted to turn to look back at the Colonel to gauge if this was true. I knew that would be a bad idea,

"Don't look back at him, he doesn't know anything- he doesn't suspect anything. Looking back at him would make you look suspicious."

To this, Karl failed to heed my warnings, he looked back. He locked eyes for a brief moment with Colonel Stauffenberg as he was taking a drink- it was awkward, it was odd. It was exactly the kind of thing that would make someone suspicious or uneasy; sometimes it's our own curiosity and burning desire for self reassurance that propagates problems. Karl was nervous now, we both knew that his small off putting look over his shoulder meant that there was a possibility that Colonel Stauffenberg would have alarm bells going off in his head. Even so, I persisted,

"Put your tray down, go get the bread and cutlery. Colonel Stauffenberg doesn't suspect anything. Everything is fine- everything will be fine."

Karl hesitantly cleaned off his tray before depositing it neatly amongst the other dirty trays stacked in a pile eleven trays high, then he confidently meandered towards the soldier standing behind the counter who had been ladeling the soup. Looking in his direction he said,

"Random inspection, have all your staff assemble here. You have one minute."

The cook snapped into attention and blurted,

"Yes sir!"

He dropped the ladle before hurrying to the back of the kitchen to notify the rest of the crew. Immediately, four other soldiers came scurrying out and stood at attention behind the counter. Looking their way Karl blurted,

"Is this everyone? Isn't there usually a six man crew?"

Looking straight ahead, one of the soldiers announced,

"Yes sir; usually there are six of us."

Karl walked towards the soldier,

"Well then where is he?"

Obviously distressed the soldier responded,

"He is sick... he has a stomach virus."

Karl's brow furrowed in disbelief

"You mean he's drunk? Alcohol poisoning huh? I should write all of you up for this, operating at altered staffing levels due to the drunkenness of an imbecile is unacceptable. It's theft towards the Reich- absolutely unacceptable. I hope that you do not have the same eased standards that you have towards staffing as you do towards cleanliness. You all stay here until dismissed."

Then Karl walked into the kitchen under the ruse of ensuring the operations cleanliness- which was apparently working well. The kitchen was larger than I expected, the walls were white except where adorned with inordinately large swastikas, all of the equipment was a pristine stainless steel. The wall to the right was stacked with canned goods, to the left was the remnants of the bread that had not yet been served for the day, the loaves were stacked in a cascading pyramid formation. I thought to him,

"Take two whole loaves, stuff one loaf up each of your uniform sleeves. Look for cutlery, specifically spoons to help them in their tunnel digging efforts."

He looked around nervously to ensure that no one was watching him before stashing two whole loaves of bread up his sleeves. They crunched as they compacted thin enough to fit passed his cuffs, crumbs fell everywhere on an otherwise clean reinforced concrete floor. He kicked at the crumbs with his boot to spread out the evidence, then his attention turned towards finding the silverware which he found in an orderly mound by a dishwashing basin. He discreetly snatched a fistfull of spoons, first depositing the cache in his right pocket then stashing another handful in his left. Then he batted at the mounds of silverware with his hand in an effort to spread them all over so that it was not obvious that some were now missing. They clanged violently as some of the silver brushed accurturments found their way back into the wash basin and some strewn all along the floor. Before heading back into the mess hall he briefly collected himself, this small act of defiance against the Reich hit him with a shot of adrenaline because he knew that if caught, he would be shot. It felt good though- even gratifying, I reassured him,

"No one will ever know."

As he emerged from the kitchen back to the mess hall his facaded demeanor engulfed his face, his jaw muscles visibly tightened along with the rest of his facial muscles as he stood before the crew,

"You all are very lucky- the kitchen is clean. The only problem is that the silverware was left out beside the wash basin- they need to be stored immediately after being cleaned. I'm pressed for time today, otherwise I would write each of you up. Do not let this happen again- if anyone from your crew is absent because of drunkenness again then next time I won't write you up. I'll reassign all of you to the front. You're dismissed, carry on."

Karl then exited the mess hall and began to make his way towards his section of barracks to give the prisoners his newly acquired plunders. As he walked, he breathed a sigh of relief, he had done it- even more gratifying, he had got away with it. As he rounded the corner of the mess hall he heard a voice call out,

"Halt. Halt right there!"

Karl continued to walk, ignoring the command- it could not possibly be directed towards him! The voice reaffirmed,

"Lance Corporal Walter! Halt now!"

The voice was now recognizable as emanating from Colonel Stauffenberg! Karl stopped before turning around to have his suspicions confirmed, it was Colonel Stauffenberg! I thought to Karl,

"If he knows, shoot him! Plant the loaves of bread and silver on him, it's not too late to get away with this"

Colonel Stauffenberg continued,

"I saw you Lance Corporal!"

Karl rebutted in ignorance,

"You saw me? Yes I just saw you as well?"

Edging the gap between the two men Colonel Stauffenberg lowered his voice while he spoke,

"I watched you in the kitchen, I had gotten up to deposit my tray and followed you into the kitchen... Tell me, Lance Corporal, what exactly are you planning on doing with that bread and silverware you just stole?"

Karl laughed disarmingly before quickly reaching for his Luger! He just got his polished black holster unbuttoned but it was too late! Colonel Stauffenberg viciously wrapped his left arm around Karl's neck as he forced his thigh over Karl's holster- in effect making it impossible for Karl to take the gun out!

"Listen to me Karl! Are you a traitor? Are you disloyal to the Reich? Do you want Hitler dead?"

Karl increased his intensity as he tried to viciously fight off Colonel Stauffenberg seemingly for his life!

"Karl! Stop it! Stop it at once! Listen to me! I want Hitler dead! I am disloyal to the Reich! We are on the same side!"

Quickly easing his efforts at resistance Karl puzzlingly exclaimed,

"What?"

Colonel Stauffenberg carried on without yet releasing Karl from his grip,

"We're on the same side. You were just about to kill me, so I know that I can trust you. I'm going to let you go, when I do, don't do anything stupid! Is there anyone else around us? Can anyone see us?"

Looking around, Karl said,

"No, there's no one else around."

Colonel Stauffenberg let Karl escape his grasp as he whispered,

"Listen to me- Hitler has lost his damn mind! We're going to lose the war- we're all going to die! He will let us all keep fighting until we're decimated. We have to do something. We have to kill Hitler. I need people I can trust- does anyone else know about your activities?"

Karl was almost at a loss for words, he went from formulating a sloppy plan to assassinate a Colonel to now conspiring to kill the leader of the Third Reich in a matter of mere seconds. He was not sure what to think, what to say, or even if this was real. Was he hallucinating? If this was real, was Colonel Stauffenberg lying to test Karl's loyalty? Was this nothing more than a ruse to officially stitch Karl up as a traitor? It was virtually impossible to know anything for certain, so I helped him:

"Trust him. He's right- this is an opportunity to make a

difference. This is our opportunity to save millions of lives. This is our chance at being on the right side of history...

Trust him.

Trust him..."

Out of options, Karl relented,

"No one! No one knows- this is my first time ever doing anything like this. You're going to kill Hitler? Hitler has lost his mind? How..."

Colonel Stauffenberg relaxed slightly as he adjusted his uniform's collar with his only three fingers,

"*We* are going to kill Hitler. I don't know how yet; you can't speak a word of this to anyone. If you do, I'll deny it outright and have you shot. I'll be in touch with you when we know more. There are others like us, we are not the only ones that know how this damned war is going to end. We never had this conversation- have we reached an understanding?"

Karl said,

"We have an understanding."

Colonel Stauffenberg, true to his word, just simply walked away like nothing had even happened. Karl's mind was a tornado of thoughts washed in a cloud of thunderstorms at this point, but he still had sleeves full of bread and pockets bulging with silverware.

The walk from the mess hall to the barracks he oversaw seemed extraordinarily longer than usual. This was most likely to be attributed to the contraband he was smuggling, which he was able to acknowledge internally. Every Nazi he passed made him increasingly more uncomfortable. Before, these men were his comrades- now they were beginning to appear as his enemies. Even so, he was lucky in that he was met with no more interference, after about five minutes he arrived at the doors of barrack number Forty. They were left slightly ajar, just enough so that he did not have to open them any wider to squeeze past. He squinted slightly as his eyes slowly adjusted from the daylight to take in the dark dank sights of the miserable conditions inside. Sunlight peeked through small cracks of the hastily erected clapboard interior fascia, which beamed throughout the room at every which angle in a spiderweb. It provided just enough light to make the derelict bunks stacked on top of one another from wall to wall visible. Inside the bunks, were the living skeletons of soldiers, some were laying on the floor as there were not enough bunks for each man. No one acknowledged Karl's presence, most of them were indifferent to the fact that he was even there - just another shakedown they figured. Karl announced to the room,

"Do any of you speak German?"

At first, no one answered, so he repeated himself once more,

"Do any of you speak German?"

A few of the prisoners turned to face Karl, not everyone knew what he was saying. Even if any of them did speak German, they would all be hesitant to talk to the Nazi standing in the room. Karl was just about to repeat himself again when he saw a man in the corner of the room stand up,

"I speak German." he said.

Karl asked,

"Come here for a moment, I'd like to speak with you."

The prisoner hesitantly made his way towards Karl, as he came closer he asked,

"What is your name?"

The prisoner responded,

"I'm Dwight."

Karl's eyes officially adjusted to the room's lighting so he was able to look the man into his eyes. That's when I knew that I'd seen this man before! The prisoner was Dwight- the same Dwight that came into the car salesroom in my real life! He was much thinner than when I'd seen him but it was undoubtedly him! His voice, his eyes, the way he walked, everything- it was absolutely unmistakable! I felt like he somehow knew that I was a part of Karl's consciousness even though this would have been impossible. It made me feel extremely uncomfortable, I wanted to crawl out of my skin because it was too close to home. It felt like he would expose me at any moment, instead of feeling like an observer, I felt like an active participant where the risk was all too real. Karl inevitably sensed my disconcerted lack of contentment before he answered,

"Dwight- I have food and supplies for your barrack. I know you or someone you know on the camp must be tunneling out of here, I have brought you spoons that will help in your efforts. All of this... this war... these damned camps... everything is weighing heavily on my mind and my heart. I will do my best to continue to bring you food and supplies, obviously I will be turning a blind eye to any efforts to escape. This is not a trick of any sort, my intentions are pure and I'm asking nothing in return other than you do not speak to any other guards about this. If you do, I will deny your claims, no one will believe you anyway so please just accept my gestures in good faith. Is there anything else that I can do for you all?"

Dwight seemed surprised to hear this spilling from a Nazis mouth. I could tell that he thought that this was all too good to be true. As Karl removed the loaves of bread and outstretched them as an olive branch to Dwight, he was slow to take them. Once he felt the lack of the rigidity of the bread in his hands he believed Karl. He knew that this wasn't a mirage or daydream, the tangibility of the bread cemented the deal in both of their minds.

Dwight half heartedly concealed a smile,

"Water... we need water. Also, we need to know the routines of the guards. We have been timing the patrols... but if I had a watch and knew when the random searches were, I could ensure that our efforts are not thwarted."

Karl's eyes briefly wandered around the room while he thought,

"Here, take my canteen for now. Getting water for everyone will be a difficult task. As far as time, take this watch, it's accurate- patrols are hourly and random searches are conducted every seven days on a rotating schedule between barracks. So if you're searched Tuesday, next Tuesday you will also be searched but at a random time."

Dwight accepted my watch and the canteen without hesitation... that's when my connection to Karl seemed to break. Like television static, everything became rapid, loud, fuzzy, and ultimately indiscernible for a few fleeting moments. The pitch ringing in my ears was so loud that it was painful, almost like the sharp teeth of a fork gnawing back and forth on a porcelain plate. The nauseating noise persisted until suddenly it didn't, out of nowhere I felt... nothing, my vision once again faded into a black abyss.

I woke up drenched in a cold sweat, confused as to where I was. My eyes quickly darted around the room in an effort to gain my bearings. I saw an old tired lamp flickering... the couch I was laying on was a light teal, soft to the touch but the fabric bunched as a sign of it's wear... the walls were white with notable paint bulges from water leaks... the kitchen island had a cluster of junk strewn all over it; I was at my apartment. I slowly sat up, I saw stars as my own vision blurred - I sat up too fast apparently. I took three deep breaths- inhale... exhale... until the stars began to diminish. The pain I felt radiating through my body starting at my collar bone, refracting off of my knees and then ending subtly in a deep throbbing in my head reminded me that I was still alive. I felt my watch still snuggly clutched in my palm, it was warm from how long I'd been clutching it. It's rhythmic hands clicking as they peacefully swept in a mechanical certainty grounded me in the moment. My grasp on reality felt to return, that being said, I also felt like I was losing my damned mind.

Alondra came into the room, she removed one of her earbuds, I hear some sort of music spilling out from it,

"How are you feeling baby?"

I felt like complete garbage- not one to complain though, I skirted the question politically,

"How long have I been asleep?"

She looked over at the green numbers displayed above our kitchen stove,

"About six hours, that's more than a solid nap. Hopefully you will sleep tonight."

Ever curious, I continued,

"What time is it?"

She said,

"It's Three thirty-three."

I yawned,

"That is one hell of a nap. Are you going out for a run?"

She nodded as she took a sip from her water bottle,

"Yup, I'll be back right after. Will you be okay while I'm gone? Need anything?"

Seemingly reassuring myself, I said,

"I'll be okay- can you just hand me pain pills?"

She walked them over to me before kissing me on my forehead.

"I love you." I said

Her lips curled into a playful smile,

"I love you more."

I waited until she left to take another pill, I didn't want her to think that I was taking too many of them. I don't think that I was, my whole damn body just hurts so much. Having something to take the edge off is an absolute godsend. I slowly wound the crown of my watch, savoring every small click of the gears which seemed to fuel my insatiable euphoria. With the watch, and the pills- I felt like I was going to be alright. I just hoped that my road to recovery was fast; I needed to find a new job- our bills were not going to pay themselves. It's sad when you are literally having to choose between healthcare or death because of how much you know you're going to owe. It's financially crippling and morally devastating. I had no idea how much my medical bills were going to be for this whole ordeal, all I knew was that there was no way in hell that I would ever be able to afford it. The whole situation made me pretty upset, primarily because I felt like there was absolutely nothing that I could do about any of it. I had no true control over anything in my life, I felt like everything was already scripted- almost as if I was just going through the motions of life without actually living it. I was on autopilot but there was no way to turn it off. Having the memories of Karl, Dwight, Terrance, Wesley... all of them... it was utterly overwhelming; it definitely didn't help anything. I essentially had the weight of all their stresses, anxieties, successes, failures, along with every other emotion that each of them ever felt rooted deep inside of my brain. I kept repeating Dwight's words over and over in my head:

"I'm in your head. Your thoughts are mine, your feelings are my feelings- there is no you and I anymore- there's just we, us."

At the time, I had no idea what he was talking about but now it made perfect sense, which scared the hell out of me. I couldn't understand why I was picked for being the steward of this watch. I didn't know what it all meant; out of everyone on God's green Earth: why me? I couldn't decipher whether or not it was a blessing in disguise or a curse, it felt like it was a symphonic mixture of both. It was almost as if my present life was a sort of deja vu. There were subtle things that I recognized I had seen before- I felt like I should know what was about to happen, I felt like I did but I couldn't make it out. Oddly enough, it was very contenting, it was like I was exactly where I should be in my life at that exact moment. Like the universe itself was reassuring me, showing that I was on the right path making all of the right turns.

I want to tell Alondra about the dreams I am having. I know that she will believe me but she may think that I'm crazy. She would most likely think that I knocked something loose in my brain from the accident somehow. I knew that these dreams were more than dreams, they were reality, I felt it in my bones. I just don't know how to prove to her that they're real; I could let her wind the watch, then she would undoubtedly know it's real because she would experience it. I don't want to let her do this though because I don't know all of the implications of being in possession of this thing. All I know for sure, is that besides me and Karl, everyone else who had this watch died with it. I wonder if that's what connected them to the watch- maybe when they died, their souls somehow became attached to this thing? Did that mean that I would die too because of this watch- because I have it now? I have so many questions with so little answers. I felt like I was chasing a ghost as I intently gazed into the watch's convex crystal, mesmerized with each mechanical click of the long white, narrow second hand. Under my breath I muttered,

"Why me?

God, why me? What am I supposed to do? Am I supposed to do anything?"

God did not answer me, but the involuntary breathing of the watch continued to answer me audibly... click... click... click.... I felt like it's mechanical heartbeat was telling me everything that I needed to know, I just couldn't understand what it was trying to tell me. All I want to do is sleep, being conscious right now is way too painful. I'm surprised that I was not asleep already, usually the pain pills put me to sleep pretty quickly. With my free hand, I grabbed the open pill bottle and brought it up to my mouth, using just my lips, I let one pill slip through, securing it between my top and bottom teeth. I washed it down with a swig of water, but this one was just to help me sleep.

THE ANGEL'S SHARE

My reality faded from a dark nothingness into a television like static that felt like a transition into a sort of purgatory. It only lasted for a few fleeting moments, until my vision fully returned. I recognized that I was back in the barracks. I was looking through Dwight's eyes, I could already tell that his lens on the world was different from my own perspective. I felt a faint gnawing in the back of my mind that somehow, someway- Dwight knew that I was a part of his consciousness. Through Dwight I felt that same deja vu feeling- I could sense that he felt it too. Most remarkably though, Dwight was oddly hopeful despite his nightmarish situation. It was almost as if he had resigned himself to his fate, but chose to do so on his own terms. His own unrelenting terms. He knew that there was nothing more that anyone could possibly take from him. He recognized that the worst case scenario was death, but he also seemed to find a sort of freedom in death. His demise was not a finality, to him it was simply a transition almost as routine as boarding a train, from one destination to the next. Somehow he knew that his story would not end simply because his heart stopped beating.

He seemingly had the answers that we were all looking for - but how?

The other men around the room were rationing their newly acquired fresh bread. Those who didn't eat all of their shares wrapped up the remaining portions in their thin dirty blankets in an attempt to hide it as best they could. From across the room one of the men proclaimed,

"This is the best bread I've ever had! It's even better than the stuff they have in France!"

Dwight looked over to him,

"Julius, you've always had a taste for the finer things in life huh?"

Julius laughed,

"No- not really! Back home in Michigan, there is this little deli that we always went to, LaRussos. I'll tell you what, they had the best bread I'd ever tasted! They had these little cannoli things too... absolutely delicious! The worst bread I ever had was that army junk they issued to us in basic down in Fort Gordon. It was bad- everyone used to call it hardtack."

Dwight lowered his head as a smile formed across his lips,

"The Army issues that hardtack all over. I actually kind of miss the stuff- no way I'd turn down some hardtack now, that's for sure. So good old Fort Gordon huh? How did you like Georgia- Augusta, isn't it?"

Julius reminisced,

"Oh yeah, it's in Augusta Georgia. I liked it down there, it was just hot as hell! When we shipped off to France after basic I was excited to get into some cooler weather, that's for sure!"

Dwight asked,

"When did you get to France?"

Julius still chewing on his bread said,

"June 6th- we were part of the last waves to show up. Utah beach, we got on shore just before the Canadians. Have you ever been?"

Dwight closed his eyes and nodded in remembrance,

"Yeah- we got in on June 5th, just a few hours before Overlord. I parachuted in; I was supposed to land three clicks North of Sword... It didn't happen that way. I couldn't find anyone from my unit, it was a mess."

Julius commented,

"Yeah, that's what we heard too. Our squadron, the 43rd Cavalry Recon, stayed on the beaches for a bit, it was... something... I buddied up with this Canadian guy though; we found out that he could get a double ration of rum if he reported his broken right after chow. We would pour the first ration in my canteen, then break the bottom of the rum bottle. Ha they were none the wiser! It helped pass the time a bit until we were reassigned to the outskirts of the Étampes in mid August. That's where I got my first real taste of French Bread."

Dwight slowly stood up from the floor,

"I was in the outskirts of the Étampes too, but in July. We must have just missed each other. Is that where you got captured?"

Julius continued,

"No, we were heading towards Fontainebleau from the Étampes- that's when we ran into the Krauts. Those bastards ambushed us, they were dug in like ticks... they outnumbered us two to one. They even had panzers... it was a nightmare. Our Squadron and C Squadron fought for hours but they had us trapped. We tried to flank them and it worked- we were just North of the Seine River. We finally were able to push back their line... all we had to do was cross the bridge from Chartres to Dreux to link back up with C Squad. We ran into more Nazis, these guys let us pass the bridge, but it was a damned trap. As soon as we were halfway across, Nazis started coming out of the wood work... they were everywhere, we were completely surrounded. We were trying to shoot our way out, that's when I got caught by one of those damned potato mash-ers. By the time I saw it in front of me, it was too late. It exploded... then the next thing I knew, the left side of my body felt like it was on fire and I had a Kraut standing above me with a submachine gun in my face... How did you get captured?"

Dwight relented,

"I broke my leg on the jump in; I couldn't walk at all. I crawled as far as I could but never found anyone from my unit. After a while I must have passed out from the sheer exhaustion and all the pain. I woke up to a submachine gun in my face too..."

Witnessing these men talk about what happened to them was truly remarkable. They're the definition of heroes, their modest and sacrifice is beyond admirable.

Julius said,

"That's exactly why I don't trust this Karl guy... sure he gave us some stuff and said some nice words but he's still a Nazi. You can never trust a Nazi, they even backstab eachother."

Dwight interrupted,

"I agree, we don't have to trust him though. We can utilize him as a resource and see what happens. We don't really have any other options. If it is a ploy... well I don't know why they would do such a thing. Maybe to learn about our tunneling efforts? We just won't say anything to him- they most likely know that we're tunneling out of here, but they don't know where the tunnels are."

Julius said,

"You're right. Let's just use that watch he gave us to time the patrols for a day or two and not do any more digging in the tunnels until we're more confident about their schedules. That should give us a better idea as to whether or not this Karl guy is trying to stitch us up."

Dwight agreed,

"That sounds like a good plan. How much longer do we have to tunnel?"

Another man laying on a bunk pitched in,

"We're getting close- we have to be almost there at this point. I think tunnel A is our best bet. Tunnel C caved in near the middle, John has been digging it out. Tunnel B is not as far as Tunnel A yet- we have to only be three-hundred yards from the rear camp fence at this point."

Julius exclaimed,

"Tunnel A it is then! Do we need more diggers?"

Dwight interjected,

"I hope not, we're running out of people who are strong enough at this point... These spoons should help us make more headway though. We will have to check with the other barracks to see if there are any bed frames left that we can scavenge from to use as more shoring for C."

Another man with a thick British accent jumped in,

"The blokes in barracks Thirty-Three still have two full beds, some of them could be used for shoring I'm sure. I'll see if they can help us out, Thirty-Three is only two barracks down from tunnel C's main entrance point in Thirty-Five, it should be easy enough to get the boards there."

Dwight said,

"Perfect- let us know if you need any help. Make sure that you do it at night, and whatever you do: don't get caught, Harry."

Harry smartly replied,

"I never get caught."

Julius snapped back,

"Then how the hell are you here now?"

They all ironically laughed at their miserable unfortunate situation. The one thing I could tell is that these men took solace in going through an unimaginable horror together.

Together they were able to dig multiple mile long tunnels, together they were much stronger, they had each other to rely on for better or for worse. While it was obvious that Julius and Dwight were the unspoken leaders of the men, they all played an integral part in getting one step closer to their freedom. Somehow, someway they created and maintained hope in an utterly hopeless situation. It is amazing that they are able to do that. I feel like it is a direct reflection on each of their bravery. They knew damned well that escaping would most likely still end in death but they proceeded to try to do it anyway. It was basically their way of still contributing to the war; the bigger ruckus that they could create in the camp, the more Nazis were tied up in dealing with the situation. The more Nazis that they could occupy with dealing with camp issues or trying to track down escaped inmates, the less Nazis the Reich had available to fight with on the front lines. It was genius really, it was also humbling to see that after everything that these men went through: they were still fighting.

Dwight turned to Harry,

"Harry, how did you end up here? I thought you were a Duke or something?"

Harry retorted,

"Now now chap; I never said that I was a Duke. I said that I am the nephew of the Duke of Wellington. I was captured after my Spitfire was shot down; I had the misfortune of crash landing three miles South of Berlin."

Julius chimed in,

"Does that mean that you've met the Queen?"

Harry proudly exclaimed,

"Yes, I actually have had tea with the queen on more than one occasion. After the Nazis learned of my status I believe that they kept me alive to interrogate and use me as a sort of bargaining chip."

Dwight agreed,

"That makes sense, the Nazis try to exploit everything and everyone that they can."

Harry said,

"Exactly. Speaking of Nazis- where did you learn to speak German Dwight?"

Hesitantly Dwight responded,

"I'm half German, my grandfather immigrated to America just before the First World War. He taught my father, who then taught me...

Dwight got interrupted mid-sentence by the barrack doors swinging open. The light of the day peeking through made it impossible for their eyes to adjust quickly enough to see who it was. A German voice announced to the room,

"Ich habe dir alles Wasser gebracht. Ich kenne, es ist nicht genug, aber es ist alles, was ich im Moment tun kann."

I recognized immediately that it was Karl's voice, since German was Dwight's second language it took a few brief moments for me to understand what Karl said before the translation made it to me:

"I brought you all the water. I know it's not enough, but it's all I can do right now."

Dwight made his way towards Karl, he had his hand outstretched with a canteen. Now that Dwight was expecting to speak German, I could hear and understand the translation effortlessly. Dwight graciously grabbed the canteen,

"Thank you."

Karl nodded as if it were not a big deal,

"Do you still have the watch I gave you? I need it back, I will give you mine- don't worry."

I assumed that the next words out of Dwight's mouth would be 'Why'; but they were not. He seemed to know exactly why Karl needed the watch back. Dwight reached into the hidden linen compartment sewn into the waistline of his pants to retrieve the watch. He held the watch in his palm while he wound it's notched silver crown,

"Karl, do not let the evils of your past define your tomorrows. Failure has a certain degree of beauty attached to it that is ultimately undeniable. Deny this infront of others, and it will deny you infront of eternity. You know exactly what must be done.

Do not falter.

Do not run.

Calvary today is our benediction. Vindicate yourself of your transgressions through a regression to the truth. Hate lives in ignorance. Truth lives in knowledge; we, each other, are truly our own limitations.

Time is ticking."

Karl's eyes widened as his jaw hung slightly ajar before he grabbed the watch. All three of us in that time were joined in a type of interdimensional fate where we were all able to acknowledge one another's presence. Instantly my perspective shifted from Dwight's eyes to Karl's- I was back inside his mind.

Harry shouted out to Karl,

"Damn you! You bastard! You Nazi pig! You give us blokes some breadcrumbs and a little bit of water and expect everything to be cheery? You must be having a laugh! You turn a blind eye to our efforts to get out of this wretched hellhole and we're supposed to forgive you? That's a bunch of rubbish! I don't care why you're pretending to help us! Maybe you're hoping for some mercy huh mate? I just want to know one thing:

Where is God?

In all this hell, this nightmare you pigs brought us all into, where is God? Where is your sense of humanity? I pray that you bastards get the same mercy that you've shown all of us!

Tell me!

Where is God?"

Dwight quickly interjected,

"Harry- God is here now; he's never left. His presence is in all of us."

Karl didn't understand English but he was not concerned with what Harry was saying, his primary concern was getting the watch back. He reached into his left pant pocket, his hand emerged with a German made pocket watch that had black Celtic numerals and an emboldened red swastika in the middle. He handed the Nazi pagentry watch to Dwight just before exiting the barracks.

Karl kept my watch clenched in his palm; I could tell that he needed it back because Colonel Stauffenberg had requested that Karl bring him an American Hamilton 4992b pocket watch. I didn't know why Colonel Stauffenberg needed this specific watch- nor did Karl. I did however know that Karl was now on his way to meet with Colonel Stauffenberg to give him my watch. So I figured that we would both soon know. I could tell that Karl had not slept or eaten in days- he was high as a kite, strung out on Pervitin. He had been taking much more than he was previously, probably due to the stress of putting his life in jeopardy to help the prisoners. Admittedly, I didn't feel bad for Karl at all; similarly though, he didn't feel sorry for himself either. We were going to meet Colonel Stauffenberg outside of the front main gates to the camp. Colonel Stauffenberg had changed Karls orders so that he was now assigned to him and would no longer be working at the camp. Now Karl would be Colonel Stauffenberg's Chief of Staff, this was a gigantic leap in rank for any officer. That being said, Karl was more hesitant than excited because he had a distinct feeling that this promotion would be his last ever. As he strutted out of the camp's checkpoints he felt an overwhelming sense of relief that he would never have to be at the camp again. It was a living hell. A hell that was now over for Karl but still very much alive for countless people. I helped implant in Karl that his life's purpose was to free everyone imprisoned at all these camps and to disassemble the nightmarish regime of the Third Reich. I repeated his new life's mission over and over in his head. I don't know if it was the Pervitin or the stress but he relented to his new ambitions fairly quickly. This was validation to me that I had done a pretty good job in planting the initial seeds in his mind. It was also a reminder of how easily we're manipulated. Hitler's propaganda overtook the common sense of Karl's mind and millions of others, then I helped right his course. Hate seemed to be as infectious and addictive as Pervitin.

Finally, Karl made it past the camp's main entry checkpoint, hopefully for the last time. Colonel Stauffenberg was waiting for him parked upfront in an expensive polished black convertible Mercedes with the top down.

Colonel Stauffenberg barked,

"Get in."

Karl quickly hopped into the passenger's seat of the Mercedes, he was amazed with the opulence of the white leather seats.

Colonel Stauffenberg continued as they sped away from the camp,

"Do you have it? Did you get the watch?"

Karl unclenched his palm to reveal it,

"It's right here- why do we need it?"

Relieved, Colonel Stauffenberg said,

"That Hamilton watch has a stopwatch function that the others do not. We are going to use that watch as a timing mechanism for a bomb that we will kill Hitler with."

Enthusiastically Karl responded,

"How? Where? What's our plan?"

Colonel Stauffenberg lowered his voice to just above a whisper,

"I have a meeting with the Fuhrer at the Wolf's Lair in five days. We will meet with Friedrich Olbricht today in East Prussia to finalize the plan and set up the explosive. The timing mechanism is the only thing that we were missing."

Karl asked,

"How will we get the bomb into the meeting room?"

Colonel Stauffenberg continued,

"We will place the time delayed bomb in a suitcase, I will bring it into the meeting. At exactly twelve-thirty in the afternoon you will call for me on the telephone. I will exit the meeting to take the call. That will give me three minutes to take your call and exit the blast radius. The Reichsmarschalls will be there, with them dead, we will implement a succession of the government. Hermann Göring, Heinrich Himmler, Reinhard Heydrich, Heinrich Müller, and Adolf Eichmann will all be killed after General Rommel receives confirmation of Hitler's death. You will call General Rommel in Berlin to give him the news after Friedrich Olbricht calls you. As soon as the bomb is detonated, we have arranged to transmit the news of his death and the immediate succession of the government to all of the Reich. We are going to end this war, Karl."

Karl's voice cracked as he said,

"Can we really do this? What if Hitler doesn't..."

Colonel Stauffenberg interjected,

"Karl- there is no what if. Hitler will be dead. We can count on you-right?"

I reassured Karl,

"This is going to work. You are going to end the war; don't worry."

Karl said,

"Yes- one-hundred percent. We can do this. Who will be appointed leader of the Reich?"

Stoically, Colonel Stauffenberg said,

"Ludwig Beck. I will be the Ministry of War Secretary.

Doing this is the lesser of two evils. It's clear that we have lost this war. Hitler has lost his damn mind, he's slaughtering everyone, including us. We have to end this madness Karl. Something must be done and we are the only ones who can do it. We will no longer stand idly by."

Karl agreed,

"You're right... How long is it to East Prussia?"

Colonel Stauffenberg said,

"Don't worry, we will be there in no time."

The Universe Stands Behind You

Karl spent the remainder of the car ride to East Prussia in silence. I continued to reassure him that the plot was going to work. After a while, he started to believe me but he was still extremely nervous. The nerves were obviously understandable but should not get in the way of the plot. Karl was also reassured by Colonel Stauffenberg's confident calm demeanor. It's not everyday that destiny calls you, but when it does- you answer. We arrived at the Wolf's Lair complex just after ten-thirty in the morning. Karl was surprised that there was such an expansive military complex in the middle of nowhere in the woods; so was I. The security to get into the complex was beyond extensive, we had to go through five separate check points before we made it onto the complex grounds. Even more shocking was how big the complex was, it was a conglomerate of buildings and bunkers all connected by roads. It was essentially a full military base except everything was pristine. The blacktop of the roads glimmered in the morning summer sun as we drove over them. The gigantic reinforced concrete bunkers ominously loomed over us and in turn, the entire compound. We parked near building Thirty-Five, which was the guest quarters for visiting dignitaries. As we parked and exited the Mercedes Colonel Stauffenberg said,

"This is where we will be staying for the next couple of days. I forgot to ask, did you not bring anything with you?"

Karl said,

"No sir, I left everything behind. I did not have any personal effects anyway."

Colonel Stauffenberg commented,

"Well that's strange. Luckily for you, it works out. Since you've been promoted you will be needing new uniforms anyway. Once we check into our quarters, have the secretary get you new uniforms. It's easy, there is a tailor on site for such purposes."

Karl replied,

"Thank you; do you want to hold on to the watch?"

Colonel Stauffenberg said,

"No, it would make no sense for me to have such an item in my possession. You hold on to it until we meet with Olbricht for lunch today."

Karl was still amazed with the inordinate proportions and acreage of the compound. His eyes were darting in every direction in an attempt to let everything soak in.

Colonel Stauffenberg continued,

"It is insane isn't it? Try not to look around too much, you will draw attention to yourself. We want to avoid that. Come, walk with me."

Karl followed Colonel Stauffenberg towards a walking path that forked off into the woods.

Karl asked,

"When was this place built?"

Colonel Stauffenberg answered,

"Nineteen forty-one, originally it was for Operation

Barbarossa. Do not walk off of the path, we are surrounded by thousands of landmines."

Karl commented,

"This is insane… where are we meeting Olbricht?"

Colonel Stauffenberg said,

"We will be meeting in the Führerbunker at the Fuhrer's Conference room. That way we can get a feel for the space. Typically Hitler sits in the middle of the conference table facing the flags. The entry door to the conference room is directly behind him."

Karl asked,

"How will you get the explosives into the conference room? Surely they will search your suitcase before you go into the meeting?"

Colonel Stauffenberg said,

"Yes, they will. That's why I was told to plant the explosives in the restroom today. That way, he said that before the meeting begins I can use the restroom and set up the explosive. Then I can return to the meeting and wait for your call."

Karl asked,

"He said? Who is 'he'? I thought that you planned all of this?"

Hesitantly, Colonel Stauffenberg added,

"I have a voice in my head… it has guided my plans. But don't worry- they are my plans. The voice in my head… it's my voice… it's my thoughts… right?"

I could literally feel the blood drain from Karl's face, he was questioning the Colonel's sanity. This verified to me that Karl had no idea that I was in his consciousness influencing his thoughts and actions. I thought that this was crazy too, except I am living it so I know it's real. I thought to Karl,

"It's fine, he's just joking around with you."

Before Karl had a chance to even reply, from around the corner of the path he heard the unmistakable deep echoing bark of a dog. The sound of footsteps trailed the dog, then from around the corner a man emerged. The voice called out to the dog,

"Blondi! What do you see girl." That voice. It was an unforgettably treacherous voice. Karl had heard it before in countless speeches and radio broadcasts.

It was Adolf Hitler.

I felt Karl's heart begin to beat so rapidly it was as if it was going to jump through his chest! The drastic influx of blood flow increased the saturation of Pervitin coursing through his veins. Karl looked towards the voice to verify his suspicions. I didn't believe it either, but it was Hitler. He did not look like he did in all of the portraits. He looked like a frail feeble old man. His thick, swooped to the side black hair fell closer to his eyebrows with every step. His hands were trembling as if he were detoxing off of some sort of hard narcotic. His upper lip danced up and down in an involuntary trembling, shaking that stupid little patch of hair underneath his nose. He was much shorter than we both expected, probably due in part to how slumped over his back was. He looked towards Blondi, then his bloodshot eyes wandered towards our direction. Colonel Stauffenberg reached out his arm and pushed it against Karl's chest, in effect nudging him off the trail. Then he rose his right arm into that dumb salute,

"Heil Hitler!"

Karl quickly got the hint and followed suit,

"Heil Hitler!"

Refusing to advocate ridiculous racist pageantry I thought to Karl,

"This is so stupid. You're a coward for saluting this guy. You're a coward for doing this dumb little Nazi salute. You know that right, coward!"

Blondi was shockingly friendly, she ran up to us with her nose going wild. She curiously sniffed us before deciding to take a lick of Colonel Stauffenberg's pant leg. Ten paces behind Blondi, Hitler called out,

"Blondi! That is no way to greet guests. Sit girl- sit!"

Blondi sat a few steps away from Colonel Stauffenberg as Hitler continued his tired gait towards us. I thought to Karl,

"Where is his security? Should we kill him now? Let's kill him now. You could probably just give this bastard a shove, he would fall down and break his neck."

Hitler bent his trembling hand up at his elbow and let his palm limply fall up towards the sky in some sort of odd acknowledgment to the ridiculous salutes. Then he looked towards us,

"Colonel Stauffenberg, beautiful day for a walk- yes?"

The Colonel responded,

"Yes my Fuhrer, it is."

Hitler continued,

"I apologize for Blondi's lack of manners."

Colonel Stauffenberg said,

"It is no trouble at all my Fuhrer."

Hitler slightly nodded before outstretching his hand to pet Blondi. His sleeves were rolled up, exposing the inside crook of his elbows. I saw a spider web of track marks all along his arms! It was obvious that this man

has been on the other side of a needle countless times! Lord only knows what kind of narcotics he has flowing through his tired collapsing veins but it was clear that he was doped up. His eyes. They were so damn empty, not because he is a monster- he is unmistakably an extremely evil human being. But his eyes are empty because of how intoxicated he is! He is looking through us, not at us! For all he knew, he could be on a different planet living in a different dimension. Now I completely understood what Colonel Stauffenberg was talking about when he said that he was out of his mind! This guy is a damn junkie! Karl and I were both completely dumbstruck! I was expecting nothing less of this man than having thick red horns violently rupturing from his skull and a barbed devil's tail trailing his inordinately proportioned rear side. Instead, what I saw was a drug addict. An old pathetic, racist, feeble tweaker consumed by hate. My preconceived notions are exactly what most people's are, I suppose. I knew of all the unspeakable acts of horror this man committed and directed. I've seen the camps. I've smelled the blood lingering in the hot stubborn summer air. I've tasted the copper on my tongue inhaled through my nasal passages. I've smelled the haunting tinge of singed hair and flesh billowing from smokestacks of death. I felt the gunpowder slowly build up in my nose as a black plaque... I know this is an evil bastard. I expected him to be a monster. We have all been told that he is a monster. We're told that all Nazis are monsters. When we do not understand how another human being could possibly be so evil we label them as monsters. This is dangerous though, because it is dismissive of their actions. We expect monsters to be atrocious and commit unspeakable atrocities. In our yearning for understanding how this evil could be committed we cannot label them as such. Monsters do not exist. There are no monsters; there are only maleficent ideas and intents planned with malice, rooted in thick effervescent permeable hate- they're the true specters that haunt our fate. We must never ever write off abominations of humanity as simply monstrosities. Genocide, murder, crimes against humainty... they're all unforgivable actions done by people entrenched in hate. We must hold these cowards accountable and never forget what they did. As I watched Hitler finish petting Blondi and hobble away slowly disappearing in the green thickets, I felt my heart swell with disdain. Four SS Security Officers that were trailing about three meters behind Hitler walked past us both and nodded. They too then disappeared in the forest.

Colonel Stauffenberg looked towards Karl,

"We have to kill that mangy bastard."

Karl agreed,

"I wish we could have done it now. Did you know that he would be here?"

Colonel Stauffenberg said,

"I knew that he was here, but I did not expect to run into him. Come, I will show you the rest of the compound."

I woke up to the slamming of our apartment's front door. My forehead wrinkled as I yawned and wiped the sleep from my tired eyes to clear my vision. It was Alondra, she was back from her run. She took out her earphones as she took a long draw from her water bottle. It reminded me how thirsty I was. I slowly sat up as my eyes scanned the coffee table looking for anything wet that could cure my dry mouth. I reached out to a half full glass of water that must have been sitting there for a while. It tasted sort of stale, which meant that it had definitely been there a long time. While I was gulping it all down I noticed that I didn't feel any pain radiating from my collar bone anymore. I set the cheap plastic cup back down and prodded at my collar bone with my index finger... it still didn't hurt at all. I extended my arm up so that my humerus was parallel to the ground, then I hesitantly moved my entire arm in small circles. There was absolutely no pain. I stood up to stretch even more- I felt completely fine. I looked towards Alondra,

"How long were you running for?"

Alondra said,

"It was only about thirty, maybe forty five minutes. How was your nap? Are you going to be ready for your appointment?"

Confused, I said,

"It was good- what appointment?"

Alondra continued,

"It's your one-week follow up. They're going to do some more x-rays to make sure that everything is set right and make sure your stitches and everything are not infected. It's at two o'clock with Dr. Olbricht."

In disbelief I said,

"Dr, who?"

Alondra reaffirmed,

"I don't know- his name is Dr. Olbricht. That's who it says your appointment is with on the reminder sheet over here. Why does it matter? Do you want to see it?"

Trying to save face I said,

"It doesn't - I just forgot. Sorry, I'm still not all the way awake yet."

Alondra began refilling her water bottle,

"I'm going to take a shower, will you be ready to go once I'm done."

I said,

"Yup, thank you for driving me babe."

"Of course babe, I'll be right out." she said.

I maintained my composure until I heard the bathroom door shut and the shower water running. Dr. Olbricht, I thought to myself... there's no way. This could not be happening. Maybe it's just a coincidence... but that would be one hell of a coincidence. What is happening? Maybe I just already knew his name before and the

dream was exactly that- just a dream. I could feel in my bones that all of this was not a dream- this was real. Was I actually awake? I grabbed at my arm hair with my finger-tips, pulling at it all. My skin moved up with a normal elasticity showing where each of my hair's pore was connected to my skin. It stung really bad, like ripping off a bandaid... I am definitely awake. I reassured myself,

"You're awake. Everything is fine, it's just a coincidence. You're fine."

Wait... are those actually my thoughts? Is there someone else in my mind!

"No, that's impossible. No one is in your mind, relax. Everything is fine."

Out of fear, I tossed the watch onto the couch! As soon as it left my hand, I immediately felt nauseous. The world began to spin, I was going to vomit! I jumped back onto the couch to grab the watch! As soon

as it was back in my palm, I felt better... this is not good. I do not understand why my body needs this watch. I do not understand how I feel better all of the sudden. I do not understand how any of this could be even remotely possible. I took another pain pill to calm my nerves, I didn't know what else to do. I clenched my fists, closed my eyes, and lowered my head in an attempt to ground myself in the moment.

"Everything is okay. You're fine... you're fine."

Alondra called out,

"Are you ready? We should probably head out."

I opened my eyes while raising my head,

"I'm ready."

Getting inside the car was not the same painful affair it had been before when we were coming home from the hospital. I was able to fasten my seatbelt on my own without any pain at all. I looked over to Alondra from the passenger's seat,

"Thank you for coming with me- and for driving. Hopefully my appointment doesn't take too long."

Alondra said,

"Of course baby, I wouldn't miss it for anything in the world. You're my world, I love you."

I said,

"I love you too... so, weird question, but if you could go back in time and kill Hitler... would you do it?

She laughed,

"Of course I would! Kill one evil person to save millions, that's definitely worth it."

I continued,

"But what if it meant that you had to die too? Like as soon as you killed him, then you would die. Would you still do it?"

She thought for a moment before explaining,

"Well, yeah- I still would do it. Obviously dying in the process is not ideal but it would still save millions. If sacrificing my life meant saving others, then it's a no brainer. Especially in that situation. Why though? Are you planning on doing some time travel?"

I nervously laughed,

"No- I've just been thinking about it after I watched that World War Two documentary the other day. Don't you think that it's weird that there were multiple assassination attempts on him and all of them failed? I mean like maybe one failed plot, I could understand that... but four or five documented failed attempts? That just seems unbelievable."

She squinted her eyes as she looked towards me sarcastically,

"Do you think that it was... a conspiracy?"

I laughed,

"Whatever- I don't think it was a conspiracy, it is just crazy. It's horrifying how one little deranged man could convince so many people to do so much evil. It's hard to even imagine, but it all happened. It wasn't even technically that long ago. It's just so..."

She cut me off,

"Evil. Sometimes people do evil things to one another under the guise of false pretenses to promote their own twisted agendas. It's horrible, but evil is proof of goodness and divinity. You cannot have darkness without also having light."

I responded,

"I agree, but don't you think that God would step in with all of the evil that was happening?"

She continued,

"What makes you think that he didn't? We're here now aren't we? God works in mysterious ways through us all. We all have free will though. We have the power to choose our own paths. We always have a decision."

I retorted,

"I agree- but sometimes it seems like our paths are predetermined. Like, if I was on a trail that forked off to the right or left, I can choose which direction to go. Ultimately though, it's like both forks in the trail end up at the same destination. Basically what I'm saying is that it seems like all of our destinies are already predetermined. We can get there multiple ways but ultimately, no matter what- we always get there."

She said,

"I think that is true to some degree... but it's not the destination that matters- it's how we get there. Just like what you said, if you're taking a hike, the beauty is in the entire walk, not just at the end of the trail."

I agreed,

"You're right but... I don't know... I just don't understand any of this."

She explained,

"Good- you're not supposed to understand. Maybe there's not a point to anything. Maybe we're just supposed to live, learn, love, and improve each other's lives. We're here only to live, how we choose to do that is up to each of us. Our legacies are in how we choose to treat others. Be kind, genuine, and unseatbelted- because we're actually here."

I raised my head to look around, we are pulling up to the hospital.

I looked towards Alondra,

"That was fast! Will you come in with me? I mean like,

don't stay in the waiting room. Come back with me for the x-ray and stuff, I don't want to be alone."

She smiled,

"You're never alone."

Hospital waiting rooms make me feel so damn guilty. I guess it's because there are other people there who are actually dying. Some of them have much worse conditions than me but we're all there waiting to be seen by the same doctors. I feel like I'm stealing their time, when I'm called back before someone who looks worse off than I am- my heart sinks. Especially if they were there waiting when I showed up. It's another injustice that I accept for convenience. A nurse emerged from the back room draped in green tired scrubs,

"Walker? Walker Henderson?" she announced to the room.

I raised my hand as Alondra and I both stood to our feet from the dirty black pleather waiting room chairs. The underneath section of my thigh left exposed by my shorts stuck to the chair as I stood up, releasing a wet loss of suction sound: *shlurp*. The nurse looked up from her clipboard as we approached,

"Walker?"

I nodded while I said,

"How are you?"

She continued,

"Good, follow me. We're going to room three-thirty-three, it's going to be a left, another left, and then a right."

We followed her while I soaked in the wretched beige walls, old bleached white floor tiles, and bright overhead lights tucked neatly into the speckled drop ceiling tiles overhanging the corridor. The nurse opened the door to the room when we got there as she ushered us inside of it with her arm. Once we were inside she closed the door behind her,

"Okay, I'm just going to take your blood pressure, weight, and temperature. Could you step on this scale please?"

I maneuvered past Alondra around the examination table which made the small room seem even smaller with three people now occupying it. I stood patiently on the electronic scale. The numbers of it quickly jumped up from zero to one-hundred-eighty-four before settling in an equilibrium at exactly one-hundred-eighty-three and thirty-three hundredths.

The nurse said,

"Perfect, one-hundred-eighty-three pounds. Go ahead and have a seat on the exam table."

I sat down as she un-velcroved the cuff of the blood pressure monitor before slipping it over my left arm. She pumped the black rubber bladder dangling from the monitor about ten times, with every pump I could feel my pulse stronger in my arm as the cuff inflated.

"One-thirty over ninety- a little bit high." she said before uncuffing the device and easing the blood flow in my arm. She then removed a digital thermometer from her pocket and turned it on, it emitted a single high pitched beep. She leaned in towards me as she slowly sweeped the thermometer in the middle of my forehead. She discreetly whispered in my ear,

"He knows about the watch."

My eyes widened and I jolted back! Simultaneously she said,

"Perfect, ninety-eight degrees."

In an utter disbelief I exclaimed,

"What!"

The nurse winked at me,

"Don't worry, that's a normal temperature. Dr. Olbricht will be in shortly."

Once the nurse left the room and closed the door behind her I looked to Alondra,

"Did you hear that?"

Alondra looked up from her phone towards me,

"Hear what? Your temperature is fine."

I could feel all the blood drain out of my face. I know what I heard her say! What did she mean... I sat

silently wondering how Alondra had not heard the nurse. A sinking feeling that something bad was about to happen washed over me. I felt like all of this was somehow a trap! Suddenly there were two faint knocks on the door! I watched the door knob slowly turn in horror! With a mechanical clink followed by a slow creaking, the door began to sneak open! Alondra looked towards me then back towards the door! A hand affixed to a white shirt sleeve grasped the now opened part of the door that was previously hidden by the door jam! The hand pushed more forcefully against the door so that it's hinges extended fully open, the hand was attached to a man in a white coat. The man confidently uttered,

"Walker? I'm Dr. Olbricht, the resident radiologist here. It's nice to meet you."

Nothing nefarious happened. He seemed to be a normal looking doctor. He was in his late forties with quiffed salt and pepper hair. My heart was still racing through chest as I said,

"It's nice to meet you too."

Dr. Olbricht continued,

"So we're going to do some x-rays today to make sure that everything is set and starting to heal properly. How have you been feeling?"

I said,

"Up until today, I felt like I got hit by a truck... but today, I'm not feeling too bad at all."

Dr. Olbricht remarked,

"Well I'm glad to hear that you're feeling better today. Progress is always good. Are you ready to come with me to the x-ray room? You can leave your phone and anything metal here."

I looked towards Alondra,

"Can my wife come with me?"

He smiled as he looked in her direction,

"Unfortunately no- we don't want to expose her to any unneeded radiation. But it will only take a few moments and then we will be right back."

Alondra said,

"It will be okay, I'll be right here when you come back."

I reassured myself,

"Everything is fine. Everything is okay- I will be okay. Don't worry, everything is fine."

I stood up from the exam table and plastered a fake half hearted smile on my face. I gave Alondra my wallet and phone but kept the watch stashed away in my pocket.

Dr. Olbricht flashed his teeth,

"Follow me."

He led the way out of our room, I hesitantly followed.

Without breaking his stride, Dr. Olbricht asked,

"So why aren't you wearing your sling? You should be wearing your sling with an injury like yours. It's very impor- tant- it allows the bones to set better and expedite the healing process.

I remarked,

"I don't think anything is broken anymore- I feel fine. I actually feel back to normal, or at least how I felt before the accident."

Dr. Olbricht laughed,

"It's a left up here; I like your positivity but it's impossible for bones to heal that quickly. In fact, not even a cut could heal that quickly. You will see what I mean once we look at the x-rays."

He then ushered me into the x-ray room. There were expensive medical imaging machines laid strategically throughout the room. Each device was cordoned off by half walls attached to a thick plexiglass which extended to the ceiling.

He continued,

"Alright so this is going to be the easiest part of your day. All you have to do is lay there, just stay still and I'll let you know when it's done. It will only be a minute or so. Do you have anything else metal in your pockets or anything? Now is the time to remove it."

Begrudgingly, I came clean,

"I have a metal watch in my pocket... but it's my good luck charm. I have to have it with me, especially for this."

He explained,

"The magnetism of the x-ray machine will destroy the watch. It would also grossly misrepresent the x-ray itself because a metal pocket watch like that is pretty big. It will be best if you just leave it here, you will only be without for a moment- don't worry."

I rejected the idea,

"Nope; I have to have it with me... how did you know that it's a pocketwatch? I never mentioned that..."

His lips curled downward and his nostrils flared,

"Walker- you need to give that watch to me! It cannot be in there with you! I need the damn watch! We're on the same side here, kid."

I raised my voice,

"No! Hell no! Either we do the damn x-rays or I'm leaving. I'm not parting ways with my watch! It is how it is! If it's ruined, so be it! But you're not touching it- it's mine! I know who you are!"

His eyes nefariously sweeped the room, he lowered his voice,

"You don't understand. Doing this... will change everything. You must give it to me! Give it to me now! You're making a mistake! You have to trust me! Please do not make the same mistake again- I beg of you! The forces at hand here are bigger than you and I! This is fate! This is destiny! Please!"

I rebuked him,

"What are you talking about! What do you mean don't make the same mistake again?"

He hesitantly continued,

"Damn! Damn your free will! I cannot speak of it! I cannot tell you anymore! You must trust me!"

I asked again,

"What mistake?"

He slumped his head forward and softly shook it from left to right. He raised his head to speak, as he opened his mouth I saw that it was now coated in a thin layer of blood! His previously ivory white teeth were stained red! Blood began to slowly ooze from the right corner of his lips! His teeth all began to crumble from his jaw as they systematically fell out while he spoke,

"Do you not see that all of this is a cycle? How can you be so blind? We are all interconnected! The past is the future as much as the future is the past! What you do right here, right now will change the past as much as it will the present. All of our choices exist in perpetuity with the universe. This is your last chance. Do the x-ray without the watch. Give it to me and lay down on the table- I'm begging you!"

The sound of his teeth hitting the floor echoed off the walls of the room like marbles bouncing off of concrete.

The voice in my head refused to relent,

"Do not give up the watch. Just do the x-ray, keep it with you. None of this is even real, none of it is possible. You're just nervous so you're imagining all of this. Everything is fine, just do the x-ray. Lay down on the table. All of this goes away as soon as you lay down on the table and do the x-ray. All of this goes away..."

My mind cannot be wrong.

I laid down on the table. Suddenly Dr. Olbricht's tone of voice returned to normal.

"Alright, just go ahead and hold the watch in your good hand as far away from your torso as you can. I'm going to go on the other side of the wall and take the x-rays. Just lay really still, okay?"

I nodded in agreement but did not want to say anything. I heard the click of some sort of switch on the machine followed by a dull humming. I silently stared at the ceiling while trying to remain as still as I possibly could. I kept the watch with me outstretched in my palm. It began to get abnormally hot as the x-ray progressed. It was more of a dull lingering heat than a burning sensation so it was not incredibly alarming. I remained still for a few more moments- I was glad that I did not let the doctor take the watch from me. It was gratifying, I felt that in some way that I had won. The whirring humming slowly faded away and ended completely with an audible electronic beeping noise.

Dr. Olbricht then reentered the room,

"You're all done! I'll walk you back, then I'll be right over with the x-rays once they're developed."

I sat up from the table and got to my feet. Dr. Olbricht was smiling, he had all of his teeth. There was no blood anywhere, not even the remnants of a single drop. I felt like I was completely losing my mind. He was acting totally normal as we walked back to the other room. Alondra was still scrolling away on her phone when I walked in, he closed the door behind me. She looked up at me,

"Well, how was it?"

Lying, I said,

"It went... okay. He will be back in with the results in a couple of minutes. Then we can get the hell out of here."

She noticed that I still had the watch in my hand,

"Sounds good to me- why do you still have that thing?" I casually responded,

"It's my good luck charm. It kept me alive on the day of the accident."

She laughed,

"Okay, whatever you say."

She went back to scrolling on her phone. I sat on the exam table and wound the watch once again. I closed my eyes with a gratifying bliss- the watch still worked. Then I looked at the time displayed on it, two-fifty-seven. My eyes wandered towards the bland clock hanging on the wall in front of me, it displayed the time as three o'clock. I looked to Alondra,

"What time is it babe?"

Without looking up she said,

"It's three o'clock."

The watch was off by three minutes, it had always been on time before. Maybe the magnetism of the x-ray threw it off a bit. Using my index finger and thumb, I pulled up on the watch's notched silver crown to correct the time. It gave way with a satisfying click, I slowly wound the minute hand forward so that it was at three o'clock. I was interrupted by two subtle knocks on the door before it casually swung open- it was Dr. Olbricht. He was carrying large negative prints of the x-ray results.

"Well, I think we may have made a bit of a mistake- but don't worry. It's great news." he said

I asked,

"What kind of mistake?"

He explained,

"Well, these x-rays show that nothing is broken. Not even as much as a hairline fracture. So you either somehow traveled back in time, have super human regenerative healing, or we switched up the initial x-rays somehow. Obviously, the latter explanation is the most likely one. I'm sorry for the switch up, that's not something that typically happens however it's not entirely unheard of."

I was in a state of complete shock! I know that my collar bone was completely broken! This just verified that my dreams were not dreams at all! Somehow I must be in another dimension for them! I must be going back in time! I tried to act casually annoyed,

"That's unbelievable! I don't know how you guys could make such a huge mistake- this is my life we're talking about here! I guess that's why they call it a medical practice, right? Because you people clearly have no idea what you're doing! Come on baby, let's get out of here! You better not bill me for any of this crap, it's your fault, not mine!" I exclaimed

I stood up from the exam table while motioning to Alondra. I wanted to get out there as quickly as possible so that no one could ask any questions. I could not explain what is happening to me- they would think that I am out of my mind! Dr. Olbricht shrugged his shoulders and casually remarked,

"I'm sorry."

I said,

"You should be!"

Then we brushed past him, walking towards the lobby to exit. Alondra said,

"That's crazy! I can't believe that! That's a huge mistake to make! That's almost like switching someone's baby or something- crazy!"

I remarked,

"They're a bunch of idiots!"

As we got in our car, I felt like I just dodged a bullet. I watched the hospital through the rearview mirror fade off into the distance, half expecting someone to come running after us.

Our Inexorable Gambit

By the time we got home I needed a nap. Not because I was tired, but because I had unfinished business. I was ready to go forward with the plot. I now knew that all of this was real. There are millions of lives at stake, including my own. That being said, I did not want this to be another failed assassination attempt. We could not afford to have that happen. I looked up assassination attempts on Hitler online. That's when I realized that there have been a seemingly innumerable amount of attempts stemming all the way back to Nineteen Thirty-Two. I do not understand how all of these attempts failed. How could it be possible? I scrolled through the pages, looking for anything that could be useful. That's exactly when I saw Colonel Claus von Stauffenberg's assassination attempt that happened on July Twentieth Nineteen Forty-Four at the Wolf's Lair! This was the plot that I was actually living through! The black and white pictures of Colonel Stauffenberg were striking! This was unquestionably the man that I knew! That man I've seen countless times through Karl's eyes! The attempt failed for reasons that seemed unbelievable! Unexpectedly, there was a last minute change in conference rooms for the meeting because of the hot July weather. Initially the meeting was supposed to occur in the Führerbunker, instead it was then held in Building Six which was a wooden framed structure primarily used by Albert Speer. The Führerbunker was almost entirely reinforced concrete, so an explosion inside of it would almost certainly kill everyone in the room. Building Six however had windows and was not as structurally secure. The blast waves would easily be able to disperse out of the space, removing the certainty of death. This is partly why Hitler survived. Another sheer coincidence was that Colonel Heinz Brandt moved the suitcase with the bomb to the other side of the conference table's thick wooden base, effectively further shielding Hitler from the blast. It created the perfect storm for the plot to fail. They realized that Colonel Stauffenberg was involved in the attempt and the subsequent coup. The next day he was killed. I needed to find a way to prevent this from happening. I know that I cannot prevent them from moving the meeting to Building Six but I should be able to get the bomb closer to Hitler. If I can prevent Colonel Heinz Brandt from moving the suitcase to the other side of the conference table's leg then I'm almost certain that the assassination would be a success. Ending the war would save millions of lives. The last nine months of World War Two were the deadliest. Killing Hitler on July Twentieth would in effect half the entire amount of deaths that happened in the war. Furthermore, it would most likely prevent us from dropping an atomic bomb on Hiroshima. It would save the world from the horrors of atomic bombs. It would prevent the Cold War. It would prevent the domino effect that atomic weapons have had on the world. It could maybe even prevent the possibility of World War Three from ever breaking out in the future. This is my destiny, this is my fate. I have to ensure that this assassination attempt is a success. There is no other way. I took two pain pills before lying down in bed. I kept my watch clutched in my right hand. I watched the water stained ceiling of our apartment slowly fade to black as I gave way to the insurmountable weight of my eyelids.

When you close your eyes, your vision doesn't really go to black. Your vision is haunted by the slow lingering lights and sights that you most recently saw. The cones and rods of your eyes are working, delicately processing all of the sensory information that you are soaking in from the outside. Your eyelids are merely curtains to the outside world. Depending on the light, when I close my eyes I see a dim red hue that's intuitively black but speckled with minute flakes of white that are as innumerable as grains of sand in the sea. This time was different. My vision was pure black. A nothingness that you have never witnessed unless you've completely lost consciousness or died. Even the blind possess a unique proprioception composed of different shades of black and all the human senses working in overdrive that help guide them. In this abyss of darkness I have no senses of anything. There is a true nothingness that's difficult to explain unless you have lived it. It's the same abyss that I had previously witnessed through others' eyes. This time I lingered in this state of nothingness for longer than I had before. It was still. It was quiet. It was as if I no longer existed in this world or the next. There was no sense of time other than a beguiling lingering feeling that seeped deep inside of my soul. Slowly, the complete lack of light succumbed to tiny specks of white light that grew in both intensity and size. They continually snowballed until my vision was a familiar television static where shapes became somewhat discernable. The burning white lights soon drowned out the darkness, replacing it with dull shades of color. The shades of color intermittently swole to deeper hues that revealed clear silhouettes of people. My vision throbbed in bursts that got clearer and stronger with every pulse of my heart until I could once again see completely.

That's when all clarity returned to me, I could once again see through Karls eyes. We were in the Führerbunker, an unfamiliar Dr. Olbricht sat across from me at an inordinately long oak conference table in a Nazi uniform. To my left sat Colonel Stauffenberg, he had a brown leather suitcase lying flat on the table in front of him. I could tell that they had already been in the meeting a few minutes and Dr. Olbricht was speaking,

"The key is the watch, the time delay chronograph function will ensure that the bomb detonates at the right time. As long as that works, I do not see how we can fail."

I knew exactly how the plot would fail- unless I intervened. I thought to Karl,

"Tell them that we need a contingency plan. We need to also consider the possibility of the meeting being moved to a different conference room because of the July heat. Tell them that we should specifically consider Building Six as a secondary venue for the meeting."

Karl heard me but was not yet convinced. Colonel Stauffenberg added,

"We have an American navigational watch that will work perfectly- it's the Hamilton model that you requested."

Dr. Olbricht continued,

"Do you have the watch with you now? Can I see it?"

I thought to Karl,

"Let him see it, but do not let him touch it. It must stay in your possession at all times."

Karl spoke up as he removed the watch from his pocket,

"Yes, here it is. I have it calibrated perfectly and these watches are quite sensitive so I will keep it until it's time to affix it to the explosive. Then I will initiate the chronograph function for three minutes. That will give Colonel Stauffenberg enough time to take my call and exit the meeting before it detonates. We have a solid plan, but I do think that we should consider all possibilities. Hitler is extremely unpredictable; it is hot as hell in here right now. What if he wants the meeting to be held somewhere cooler with a breeze? I think that we should really account for the possibility of the meeting being moved due to the heat. I think that the most likely alternative would be Building Six."

Dr. Olbricht stroked his chin with his thumb and index finger,

"That's a good point. If the meeting is held in a room with windows then the blast energy will dissipate much faster and at a higher rate. Especially if we were in Building Six- that place is nothing more than a wooden shanty. We must place the suitcase as close to Hitler as we can."

Colonel Stauffenberg said,

"That shouldn't be an issue. I will be able to get the suitcase very close."

I thought to Karl,

"Warn them that the blast could be further shielded if moved near the table's leg. Most of these conference tables are extremely thick and gaudy."

Karl listened to my advice,

"Good- I don't think that getting the suitcase close enough will be an issue. The only issue I can foresee is if the suitcase is moved or kicked aside. Especially if it's moved to the side of the table leg. These damned conference tables are solid wood. If the bomb is on the other side of the table leg then it could act as a shield."

Colonel Stauffenberg agreed,

"That's a good point- but that will be out of my control. If someone moves the suitcase aside and then I move it right back, it would be very suspicious. Also, I will be out of the room while it detonates so there's no way that I could even know if someone moved it somewhere else in the room after

I've left. Either way, I'm extremely confident that with a bomb of that size in any room, there will be no survivors."

Karl interjected,

"We cannot assume- we do not have that luxury. We must be sure! I can bring the suitcase into the meeting... I can see it through to ensure it stays as close to Hitler as possible."

Dr. Olbricht said,

"That's not necessary- the bomb will work. That's exactly why we're using the watch as the time delay mechanism. We could have gone with the acid capsule, but since it has to eat through the wire to initiate the primer pin there are too many variables. That's why the bomb on the train in Russia failed. External factors have an effect on the reaction and timing of the bomb- if it even goes off. For the train bomb, the acid ate through the wire and the primer pin went off but failed to detonate the bomb, probably because it was below zero. With the time delay, we control all aspects of the explosion."

Colonel Stauffenberg continued,

"Fate has offered us this opportunity- we must not squander it. Karl, we will stay with the original plan. It will work. There's no way in hell that it will not. Destiny is on our side here, I promise you. After the bomb goes off, Karl, you and I will fly to Berlin. I will initiate Operation Valkyrie once in Berlin. Do either of you have any questions?"

Karl and Dr. Olbricht both looked at each other before shaking their heads from side to side. Dr. Olbricht said,

"No- we're ready."

Colonel Stauffenberg said,

"Good- then it is settled. Olbricht, leave the explosives with us, we won't talk to you until the Twentieth. I will see you in Berlin my friend."

Dr. Olbricht exclaimed,

"Long live our secret Germany! I will see you in Berlin. Godspeed men."

He then casually stood up and excused himself from the room. Karl began to feel a sensation of water dripping on his forehead. He wiped his brow before looking back at his hand to check what the substance was. There was nothing there. The dripping continued, I could feel the droplets steadily collide with his skull as they bursted and splashed into his eyes. Again he wiped his brow- but there was nothing there. Colonel Stauffenberg noticed his strange behavior,

"What's the matter?"

Karl looked up towards the ceiling,

"Water, there must be a leak, there's water dripping all over me! Colonel Stauffenberg fixed his gaze up on the ceiling before returning his eyes towards Karl,

"There's no water, WALKER!"

I was immediately stunned! My eyes ripped open, instantly waking me! My forehead was wet! The ceiling above my bed was water bulged and bleeding a steady drip of water! I ferociously wiped off my forehead before looking at my bed- it was soaked.

"Damn it!" I yelled

Alondra came running into the room,

"What's wrong... oh, damn it! I hate this place babe!"

I seconded her,

"I hate it too! Will you call the maintenance people? I'm going to try to finish my nap on the couch, I'm tired as hell."

She said,

"Yeah- I doubt they will come though. They're literally worthless."

I agreed,

"I know, that's all we can really do though babe. Thank you. You want me to grab a bowl to catch the water? I think we have that big red one under the kitchen counter by the stove."

She said,

"No, I got it. I'll wake you if I need anything."

I said,

"Sounds good, thank you babe."

I took another pain pill to make sure that I fell back asleep before settling into the couch. I don't understand how Karl was feeling what I felt. The lines between our realities are really beginning to blur. There's no way that Colonel Stauffenberg actually said my name. He must have just said "water" and it must have sounded like "Walker" to me. I'm nervous that I might miss the whole plot, I can't miss this! It's my destiny! Clamping my eyelids shut I tried to force sleep. This only made the doubts in my mind whirl around faster, with a raging calamity. All of the 'What ifs' were haunting my soul. Each lingering doubt hung off of me like an anchor, suspending my consciousness in a sleepless limbo. Sometimes it's not the things that you don't know that plague you the most; instead, it's everything that we *think* that we know. My soul feels so old, like a tired varnished leather. It was as if I am carrying the sins of every person who had the watch before me on top of my own. The weight is utterly crippling. In an attempt to quiet my mind I began counting each click of my watches second hand in my head.

When my vision returned, I quickly realized that I was looking through Karl's eyes. I am back. I was not in the meeting anymore. Somehow in the short amount of time I was awake, a few days had elapsed! I could sense that Karl is unusually nervous. Today is July Twentieth, today is the day! I thought to Karl,

"Check the time!"

He looked down at my watch, it was ten twenty-one in the morning. Karl is waiting for Colonel Stauffenberg to bring the bomb so that it can be armed. We impatiently waited for him. Karl was ready but scared, which is more than understandable considering the stakes. I tried to reassure him,

"Everything is going to go as planned. It will all be okay. In a matter of hours, we will be on a plane to Berlin. Hitler will be dead. The war will be over. We are okay. Everything is exactly as it should be."

Colonel Stauffenberg opened the door to Karls quarters and locked it behind him. Karl looked to the watch then back up to Colonel Stauffenberg,

"Ten twenty-seven, you're early."

Colonel Stauffenberg gently placed a black leather suitcase on the table,

"Are you ready?"

Karl answered confidently,

"I'm ready."

Colonel Stauffenberg opened the suitcase to reveal two white square bricks of plastic explosives,

"Let's do this then. All we have to do is insert the primers into the charge and then attach the watch to the main primer. Do you know how to use the stopwatch function of the watch?"

Karl said,

"Yes, I can initiate it whenever you're ready."

Colonel Stauffenberg inserted the primers into the explosives,

"Okay, set it for two hours and five minutes. That way I'll have plenty of time to get out of there by the time you call for me."

Karl lifted the watch's crown with his thumb and index finger and then rotated it clockwise two hours and five minutes.

Colonel Stauffenberg continued,

"Perfect, now unscrew the back case of the watch. You need to attach the positive and negative primer wires. First, attach the negative to the mainspring. Then carefully attach the positive to the dial train. This will complete the circuit;

once the time expires, the dial train will move the minute hand one last time which will detonate the bomb."

Karl intricately followed the instructions, it did not instantly explode so I'm assuming that it worked. Karl affixed the watch to the plastic explosive and closed it all into the suitcase. I thought to Karl,

"You need to convince him that the meeting is going to be in Building Six. Insist that you plant the bomb in the bathroom of Building Six- that way it will be hidden and ready to retrieve."

Karl said,

"I will plant the bomb. It is not official yet but I know for fact that the meeting is going to be held in Building Six. It's not going to be in the Führerbunker. You have to trust me on this."

Colonel Stauffenberg stared at Karl,

"I don't know why- but I think you're right. You better be right Karl. Since, as of now, the meeting is still in the Führerbunker there shouldn't be any sentries at Building Six. Go now and plant the bomb, as soon as you're done meet me in my office. Bring me back my suitcase."

Karl nodded,

"I'll see you soon."

This was not Karl's first time traveling with contraband but this time he was smuggling something deadly. As Karl walked to Building Six I could feel his cheeks grow red and the sweat pool in the middle of his back on his undershirt. It was partly because he was nervous, but mainly because he was so strung out on Pervitin and the midday July sun was cooking him. It was much hotter walking on the pavement but he stuck to the course to minimize jostling the bomb around in the suitcase. When walking with a bomb, smooth pavement beats uneven dirt terrain anyday. The heat did work in his favor though in that there were not a lot of other people walking around the compound. Considering the fact that all

Nazis go to hell, it's ironic that they choose to minimize their time out in the heat. It's also just another indicator that they too are human; extremely flawed, racist, murderers- but still human nonetheless. Colonel Stauffenberg was right, there were no sentries posted at Building Six. Karl breezed past the wooden door to the structure and took his first right around a blind corner. Then he went left, directly into the bathroom, locking the door behind him. He briefly looked around to ensure that no one else was there- it was empty. He methodically removed the bomb from the suitcase before placing it in a small hutch underneath the window. He delicately pushed the bomb towards the back of the hutch, until he felt the resistance of it pushing on the back. He stacked the toilet paper stored in the hutch into a pyramid to shield the bomb from view. It was a perfect hiding spot in that it was so obvious a space that no one would really think to look there unless they already knew. Karl was about to make a hasty exit, I thought to him,

"Check the toilets, make sure that they're stocked with toilet paper so that no one goes looking for more."

It's always the small details that get most people caught. He checked each of them- they were stocked up. He glanced around the room one last time before unlocking the door and exiting, with Colonel Stauffenberg's suitcase in tow. He peeked his head just past the doorway of the conference room, there were five windows against the back wall. To his right, there was a smaller oak table with seating for three directly underneath another window. The main oak conference table stood ominously in the middle of the room, it was big enough to seat at least twenty people. We both appreciated in awe the enormity that this nondescript wooden room would play in history. This would be the place where Adolf Hitler's reign of terror ended. Karl then turned around and exited Building Six. Not a single soul other than me saw him plant the bomb, it is perfect. Karl made his way towards Colonel Stauffenberg's office, this time avoiding as much of the pavement as he could. Karl felt a sense of relief that so far everything was going as planned- so did I. I am surprised that I still had a connection to Karl's consciousness. In the past, whenever someone was out of possession of the watch, I lost the direct connection to their consciousness and was only left with their memories seared into my mind. Maybe this time it was different because of the deep innate connection that Karl and all of our fates had with the watch. Either way, my bond in his mind seems permanent. Karl got to Colonel Stauffenberg's office fairly quickly. He knocked three times on the door, there was a small pause before a voice on the other side hollered,

"Come in, it's open."

Karl walked into the office,

"It's done. I put it in the back of the hutch underneath the window. You will have no issue finding it."

Before Colonel Stauffenberg could respond, his desk phone began to ring. They both looked towards the phone as if they already knew exactly what the purpose of the call was. Karl gave Colonel Stauffenberg a nod signaling for him to answer it- he did.

"Hello - this is he... yes... that's correct. Building six- got it. Thank you."

Colonel Stauffenberg looked up towards Karl,

"The meeting will be in Building six. I don't know how you knew- but you were right. Are you ready to do this?"

Karl confidently replied,

"Yes- there is no time better than the present. Let's kill Hitler. Let's end the war."

Colonel Stauffenberg stoically nodded,

"Once you call me, wait until I actually answer the phone. If I answer and say 'It's hot' then there is an issue and the plan is off. If I say 'I will see you in Berlin tonight' then everything is going as planned. Immediately pick me up from Building Six in the car, I will be waiting for you up front."

Karl said,

"I understand- everything will go according to the plan. Godspeed my friend."

Colonel Stauffenberg nodded and shook Karl's outstretched hand,

"I'll see you on the other side."

Destiny's Circle

Karl sat impatiently behind Colonel Stauffenberg's desk waiting for the minute hand of the clock to strike six. He popped another Pervitin in his mouth, chewing it. It crackled between his back molars briefly until the pill gave way to it's ultimate powdery form. He raked the powdered remnants back and forth with his top and bottom incisors before letting it all settle on his tongue. It had a deep sour taste; almost like if you rang out all the alkaline properties of a battery and swished it around in your mouth. It burned at first. Then the burning gave way to a tingling that faded to an artificial numbness. That numbness then radiated from his mouth outwards, taking complete effect on his entire body. He closed his eyes and swallowed the chemical cocktail. His heart thudded in his chest like an angry thunderstorm. I could feel and hear his increasing pulse rhythmically echo in his ears. When he opened his eyes his vision was clouded by a myriad of stars that seemed to burst across his corneas like lightning. The lights gave way until we could once again see 'normally' but we were looking through a distorted lens. It was an intoxicated lens that dulled everything but somehow was disgustingly gratifying. Inside, his organs clawed at themselves in a battle with the foreign substance that was undoubtedly killing him. Even so, he seemed to be at peace with his addiction. It was mortifying to see. Suddenly, his stupor was shockingly interrupted by the phone ringing! He looked at it for a few brief moments, trying to decide what to do. He picked it up off the receiver as he hesitantly held it to his ear. The voice on the other end said,

"Karl, you cannot change the past."

I knew that voice. The voice is my voice! I began to panic! Wake up! Wake up- I thought to myself. The receptors of Karl's brain were completely fried! I couldn't rouse myself back to consciousness! Karl demanded,

"Who is this! What are you talking about!"

My voice continued,

"What's happened is done. There is no changing it. You can try, you can push against the past but the past will push back harder, Karl. Everything is exactly as it is supposed to be. Don't you understand that you're running around in a circle of time? You have been here before, you have already done all of this a thousand times. You're living in repeat."

Karl slammed the phone back into the receiver and jumped up to his feet! He was just as confused as I was! He paced the room viciously in a deep preponderance of the situation. He looked up towards the clock- it is twelve twenty-five!

"Damn it! he yelled

I tried again to wake up, I envisioned myself opening my eyes and lurching up out of bed. It was pointless though, I was not going to wake up. I am stuck inside of Karl's mind! I tried to calm him down in an attempt to also calm myself,

"Relax- that didn't happen! You imagined it! You haven't slept in days and you just took another Pervitin. It was just a hallucination. Everything is fine. Everything is going to plan. There's only a few minutes until all of this is over. Breath.

Watch the clock, it's almost time to call. Relax- be calm. We got this."

From the corner of Karl's eyes I saw a dark silhouette. Karl saw it too! He looked over to the corner of the room- a dark plume of thick black smoke loomed. It manifested itself slowly, hauntinly, into the shape of a man! Karl batted at his eyes in an attempt to make the vision go away- it didn't. The silhouette was real! The clear outline of a man, approximately six and a half feet tall emerged as the smoke wafted off into the ground! The middle of the silhouette was entirely translucent but it was clear as day- it was a man! His black outline radiated in a thick dark haze that lingered silently in the air like a cloud of flies! Karl yelled at the entity,

"What do you want! What the hell do you want from me? You bastard!"

He violently ripped out his luger from his tired leather holster! He fixed the pistol on the shadow as he quickly squeezed the trigger! Two shots rang out- our ears instantly began to buzz in a haunting ring! The shadow stayed motionless standing in the corner. The two bullets left small holes in the wall behind it where the daylight now peeked through. Karl yelled again,

"What do you want!"

Karl's eyes looked towards the clock, as if it were engulfed in flames, the whole clock began melting off of the wall! It steadily dripped to the floor in a thick burning goop!

"Damn it" he exclaimed

I thought to Karl,

"Call Colonel Stauffenberg now!"

Karl dropped his Luger on the desk and reached out for the phone. He methodically dialed the extension for building six, an operator answered.

"Operator, how can I direct your call?"

Karl announced impatiently,

"Building Six, Colonel Stauffenberg!"

The operator said,

"One moment."

The phone began to ring. After three rings the call was answered, the voice said,

"Building Six communications, this is Hans. Who's this?"

Karl slowed his breathing and calmed his voice,

"This is the Chief of Staff to Colonel Stauffenberg. I need to speak with him immediately, it's urgent."

Hans said,

"He's currently in a meeting with the..."

Karl interrupted,

"Damn it Hans! I know he's in a meeting with the Fuhrer! This is urgent! get him now!"

Han's hesitantly murmured,

"Hold the line."

Karl fixed his eyes on the shadow figure in the corner of the room. It still stayed completely motionless. Colonel Stauffenberg's voice finally came on to the other end of the phone,

"Karl? I will see you in Berlin tonight- yes?"

Karl said,

"It's watching me."

Colonel Stauffenberg said,

"What?"

Karl continued,

"It watched me. It watched me call you. It watched me the whole time."

Colonel Stauffenberg reasserted,

"I will see you in Berlin tonight- yes?"

Karl said under his breath,

"Yes."

The phone line went dead. Karl looked back up at the clock- somehow it was normal again. It read twelve thirty-three; he picked up his pistol and pointed it back at the shadow. He then walked heel to toe backwards out of the office. He watched the door close, letting the figure disappear behind it. Instantaneously he heard the blast of the bomb. He felt the shockwaves deep inside of his chest. Even though he knew it was coming, it still startled him. He hurried into the car to make his way to Building Six, it would only be a minute drive. With how crazy the last thirty minutes had been he was hesitant that the key would even start the damned thing. Even so, he slipped the brass key into the ignition and twisted it. The car started with any issue, we were both very relieved. Things were unfolding extremely fast, which worked to our advantage slightly because it left us both with less time to think about what was really happening. As we pulled up to Building Six we could see smoke billowing from the windows of the conference room. Colonel Stauffenberg was waiting outfront as planned. As we pulled up, we could hear the sirens roar from approaching ambulances. Colonel Stauffenberg jumped into the passenger's seat,

"Drive! Let's get out of here!"

Karl exclaimed,

"Is he dead?"

Colonel Stauffenberg said,

"He has to be. There's no way anyone in that room survived."

Karl retorted,

"I hope that you're right."

Colonel Stauffenberg continued,

"What the hell were you talking about on the phone?

Karl looked over his shoulder before answering,

"I don't know- there was a figure in your office... some sort of specter. The clock began to melt... something supernatural is happening."

Colonel Stauffenberg asked,

"Are you taking Pervitin?"

Karl said,

"Yeah, but that has nothing to do with it.

Colonel Stauffenberg exclaimed,

"Damn it! You're hallucinating! You fool! Can you still drive? We need to get to the airport."

Karl sheepishly blurted,

"I'm fine! I'm not hallucinating, I'm fine!"

We were getting close to the main exit. Colonel Stauffenberg said,

"You need to relax, act natural. Let me do the talking."

We pulled up to the gate and a sentry armed with a submachine gun approached casually,

"Unfortunately you guys cannot get through. A landmine up the hill went off or something. I have orders that no one can enter or exit."

Colonel Stauffenberg said,

"Well I'm late to a meeting with Himler. You must let us pass."

The sentry postured defensively,

"The orders are that no one enters or exits. You're not going anywhere Colonel."

Colonel Stauffenberg raised his voice,

"You damn imbecile! Who's your commanding officer? Get him on the phone at once!"

The sentry hesitantly said,

"Colonel Gruber... I'll phone him."

He walked back to the guard shack and dialed the phone. Colonel Stauffenberg shouted out,

"Let me speak to him!"

The sentry walked the corded phone out and handed it to the Colonel,

"This is Colonel Stauffenberg, we had breakfast together this morning- remember. Yes, well one of your men will not let me pass- I'm late for a meeting with Himler, I need to go now.

Please tell this man to let us pass. Thank you- (he lowered the phone from his mouth) Colonel Gruber says to let us through."

The sentry refused,

"I need to hear that from Colonel Gruber myself."

Colonel Stauffenberg yelled,

"Damn you! Come take the phone- hear it for yourself!"

The sentry took the phone, he listened for a moment. Then he nodded and raised the barrier arm. We drove through, exhaling a sigh of relief as soon as we were a few hundred yards away. On the way to the airfield I couldn't help but feel absolutely helpless. I wanted proof that Hitler is dead. Without some sort of evidence, it was obvious that we were repeating history and that we hadn't changed a thing at all. If Hitler is still alive then Operation Valkyrie would be implemented too early by young eager officers. Colonel Stauffenberg and I wouldn't get to Berlin for another three hours. We would be cut off from communications on the ground, believing Hitler to be dead. Once in Berlin, we would continue to think that everything went to plan until we met with Olbricht. We would then learn that there were some survivors from the meeting; it would be the first time we realize that Hitler could have survived. Hitler would hold a radio broadcast, effectively ensuring that all orders from Operation Valkyrie are immediately reversed. We would be detained by the SS and executed in an alley in Berlin tomorrow morning. That is how our lives would end. That would be the end of our story. The course of history would remain charted- millions of more innocent lives would be lost. Nothing would change. I always thought that knowing the future would be liberating- it's not. It's somewhat torturous because you know exactly what will happen so you're effectively nothing more than a spectator. It removes all of your freedom. It puts you in a box; you're stuck. Knowing that you're imprisoned by the universe makes you feel as if you're damned by fate. I hope that Hitler is dead.

As we boarded the plane to Berlin, Colonel Stauffenberg was visibly confident about what had just occurred. Karl was too, I did not let my truths bleed through into his. Afterall, I didn't know if Hitler was still alive or not for certain. Either way, it would only be a matter of time until we all knew. As Karl settled into his seat I thought to him,

"Ask about the placement of the bomb. Was it far enough from the table leg but still close enough to Hitler?"

Karl was so strung out that I had to repeat my thoughts to him over and over again. He eventually got the message and spoke up,

"How far was the bomb from the table's leg?"

Colonel Stauffenberg answered,

"It was close to the table's leg- touching it actually. But it was on Hitler's side. Relax, he's in half a dozen pieces in hell right now, I imagine."

Karl nodded with satisfaction as they began to taxi out to the runway. As the plane began to rapidly accelerate, Karl's arms began to feel numb. He was not alarmed at all by the sensation, but I definitely was. As the plane left the ground and climbed in elevation, the sensation became much stronger. The numbness radiated from deep in his bones, the feeling slowly began to overtake his whole body. His vision began to shake and was flooded with small specks of light. It became obvious that he was about to lose consciousness. He still was not alarmed- he was completely calm. I am nervous as hell! If he loses consciousness, what happens to me? Will I remain connected to him? Will I finally wake up? Will my existence be erased entirely? Would my physical body be in a coma while my consciousness continued on like a drifter in others? I am in a sheer panic! Karl closed his eyes, resigning himself to his state of unconsciousness. My perspective from Karl's vision immediately was severed. My vision seemed to float freely from Karl's into a third person point of view- I was now in the middle of the plane. I am having a complete out of body experience where I am nothing more than a spectator. It is as if I am an orb of light moving seamlessly through time and space. I cannot choose what direction I look, everything is visible though. I have a three-hundred and sixty degree view of everything at once. It's impossible. I can see Karl slumped over with his head hanging forward in the seat. I can see Colonel Stauffenberg peering out of the plane's window. I can see the entire plane cutting through the brisk blue sky. I am everywhere and nowhere at once. My orb of vision begins to float down towards the ground at a constant rate of speed that must seem much slower than it actually is. It's obvious that my trajectory is an unnatural diagonal angle towards the Earth's surface. None of this is possible, yet here it is. Here I am. Soaking in an unreasonable amount of visual sensory information in an incongruent cosmology. I want to desperately deny that any of this is real- but I cannot dispute it. Suddenly I'm hovering a mere hundred feet above the ground. I can see the conglomerate of concrete structures that compose the Wolf's Lair. For some reason, my consciousness is gravitating back. I'm heading directly towards a thick cloud of filthy smoke that's looming ominously, almost still in the air. Before I even realize it, I'm in the middle of all the smoke. Then I'm surrounded by a heap of wreckage and rubble. I can make out the silhouettes of bodies laying mangled around the room. I recognize that I am in the Building Six conference room! My vision stops directly above the watch laying on the floor face up! It is still pristine, there is a thin layer of dust coating it's crystal but it's still working! It still has the primer wires dangling from it's exposed back. About three feet from the watch, there's a man laying face down on the ground. I can see his back slowly rise and then fall as he draws each breath- he's still alive. The man visibly struggles to lift his head up, but after a few moments, his chin is parallel to the ground. He has an unorderly glop of black hair swooped over his face, he methodically reaches out to paste his hair back to his soot covered head. That's when I saw the whites of his eyes emerge from his ash covered face - everything fell into place. I recognized that stupid haircut- the small patch of hair clinging on for dear life to his upper lip, his cowardly empty eyes. The man is Hitler. Somehow he survived the blast. Using his finger tips, he inched his body forward towards the watch. He saw the wires dangling out of it and must have known that it was the detonation device. His whole hand trembled ferociously as he reached out for it. My vision tunneled into the watch, as soon as he touched it, everything faded to a deep white alabaster.

Most of the time fear is projected outwardly as anger. Rejection is quickly transformed into despair, which then morphs into blame. Anger mixed with blame and despair transforms self hatred into hatred towards others. The human psyche will not allow itself to think that there's 'something wrong with us'; instead, there has to be something wrong with someone else. Our problems cannot be our own doing- it has to be someone else's fault. In the mind of a megalomaniac there is no right and wrong. It's impossible for someone that flawed to comprehend that their problems are theirs alone. Their only truth is what they decide it to be. They will tell themselves whatever they need to hear to justify exactly why their beliefs are right. They feel in their bones that they're righteous. Righteousness is the most fatal pill that anyone could ever swallow. It makes someone believe that their pursuits, no matter what the cost or implications, are divine. It comes to a point where the "righteous" are brainwashing themselves that they are actually divine. Righteousness, false divinity, and the belief that we are owed something by this world is the holy trinity of evil. It's the omnipotent cocktail that has fueled genocides, wars, and innumerable injustices. Self proclaimed omniscient demigods can do no wrong in their eyes because their ambitions are fueled by the divine. This is exactly how it is in the mind of Hitler. He's nothing more than a coward- a frail, drug addicted spineless man. He truly believes that his dastardly vision for the world is the right path- in his mind it's the only path. I could tell that he used the multiple times that he escaped death as valid evidence that he is divine. It started in the trenches of WWI. He believes that he heard a voice in the trenches telling him to move from his position, seconds later, a mortar shell landed where he was- it killed all the soldiers there, except him. This was just one instance he used as clear evidence charting his clear dichotomy between this world and the next. He believed that he couldn't die. Even so, he is extremely scared of everything- he's suspicious of everyone. He wears bulletproof jackets, never takes the same route twice, employs body doubles, and never follows the same routine. He makes every effort to make his actions entirely unpredictable. For a man who believes he cannot die, he sure as hell acts like he can. Inside this man's mind, it is an extremely dark, lonely, desolate, and damned destination. At first, I was inundated with a deluge of all his fragmented memories. Everything was in bits and pieces, almost like a movie reel that has been split with a dozen movies. His mind only remembers things that are either entirely in his favor, or entirely against him. Like how he remembers his father Alois Hitler. He was a customs agent that was as promiscuous as he was abusive. He died when Adolf was fourteen-years old. The primary memories of his father are that of him beating him and his mother. He hated him; once he was dead, he was able to pursue his desire to be a professional artist. As an artist, he was very partial to architectural paintings and renderings. This drew him to Vienna's Academy of Fine Arts, where he subsequently failed the entrance exam twice. He blamed failing the exam on the fact that the leaders of the academy were Jewish. He reasoned with himself that it was the school's Jewish leaders that conspired against him and excluded him from attending. In reality, the sole reason was that as a subpar artist, he failed the entrance exam. Already, even as a young man, his faulty egocentric thoughts dominated his mind. His own flawed logic fueled his anger in an internal cycle of fear, self hatred, and lack of competency. While living in Vienna, he tried to sell paintings on the streets and often worked as a day laborer to scrape by after the money his father left him ran out. As a result of him being broke, he joined the Sixteenth Bavarian Reserve Infantry Regiment as an infantryman in Nineteen fourteen. During his time as an infantryman, his primary role was that of a dispatch runner for the regimental headquarters. He intensely glorified the role both to himself and the world, but in reality, on the battlefield this job was known as a "rear- area pig". All of his memories from the war were grandiose to such fabled proportions that I could tell he even had a difficult time believing it. During the end stages of the war, he was exposed to mustard gas which resulted in a variety of injuries. He was hospitalized because of them; when he learned that the war was over he put himself into a deep hysteria that induced a temporary psychosis initiated blindness. He found antisemtic literature that seemingly verified his own horrific beliefs and used that as a basis to his cruel ideology. The way he felt now was similar to how he felt after being exposed to the mustard gas except this time it is worse. I can feel his intense confusion. Some of it is brought on by the explosion he was in, but a lot of it is the fact that he's high on a cocktail of drugs. His doctor, Dr. Morell, has been steadily keeping up with his request to pump him full of powerful narcotics. It is to the point that he has no veins good enough to inject into his arms anymore because of all the scar tissue. He is a dope fiend. A frail hateful coward.

Nothing more than a sad pathetic man. He is laying on the ground choking on the smoke of the fire. Most of the pain he is feeling is radiating from his right ear and his legs. The blast covered him with shrapnel and punctured his eardrum. Barely audible over the incessant ringing he can hear a voice call out,

"Fuhrer! Mein Fuhrer!"

He doesn't have the wherewithal to respond. I can see two Nazis in gas masks approach him; he's still in such a state of confusion that he puts up no resistance at all as they bring him up to his feet by his arms. The two Nazis are murmuring words that are inaudible in their gas masks and over the crackling of the fire, disorienting billowing black smoke, and the glass shattering humming in his ears. Suddenly he can feel the distant radiating heat of the sun replace the heat of the fire on his face. His weight is still entirely supported by the Nazis on his right and left propping him up. Without them, he would fall into a heap on the cement. The brightness of the day blinds his bloodshot dust covered eyes- he shuts them. Using both of his palms he bats at his eyes in a circular rubbing motion in an attempt to remove the debris. His efforts are interrupted by his legs being picked up from underneath him- I can tell that he's being placed on a stretcher. He still cannot fully comprehend anything. Even so, he's completely docile to being lifted. He's hastily loaded into a medical evacuation vehicle. Three Nazis loom over him,

"Mein Fuhrer- can you hear me?"

Hitler doesn't respond, but he can hear him. The Nazi repeats himself once more,

"Can you hear me?"

He waves his hand above Hitler's face; he instinctively swipes it away. He's still extremely confused and becoming increasingly agitated. Sadistically, I enjoyed seeing this bastard in the amount of pain he is in. I know that it's wrong to revel in the pain of anyone but with this man, I feel like it's warranted. The pain from his burst eardrum began to flourish as whatever adrenaline he had left in his system began to steadily wear off. He clutched his ear in pain before exclaiming,

"Morell! Where is Dr. Morell? Get me Morell at once!"

One of the Nazis spoke up, a balding man with a rounded chubby jowls and pop bottle glasses spoke up,

"I'm here Mein Fuhrer! We're taking you to the infirmary right now! I will be able to assess your health better there. Do not worry- you're in good hands."

Hitler cried out,

"I need an injection now! I can't wait until the damned infirmary! Now!"

He kicked his legs about up and down on the stretcher and waved his clenched fist sporadically! His trousers are completely tattered so his dungeon white chicken legs poke through them more and more with every flail. His blood ran in spiderwebs down the visible portions of his legs from debris hanging out. Everytime he smashed his limbs back on the stretcher I could feel the debris dig deeper into his rotten flesh. Dr. Morell clamored to find a syringe and bottle of morphine. Hitler cried out again,

"Hurry it up!"

Dr. Morell's breathing became so heavy that it was audible; he stabbed the needle end of the syringe into the vial of morphine. He rapidly pulled back on the plunger of the syringe, drawing the drug into the barrel with suction and gravity alone. He called out to the other Nazis,

"Tie off the Fuhrer's left arm!"

One of the Nazis quickly rolled up Hitlers sleeve and then proceeded to tie a black piece of rubber tubing around his arm. I could feel Hitler's pulse throb as his blood pooled from the rubber tubing's pressure. Dr. Morell drew in closer to Hitler, soothing him with the sight of the syringe just like how a mother soothes her baby with the sight of a warm bottle of milk. Hitler was acting so childish I half expected Morell to say,

"Okay- here comes the airplane!"

as he snaked his fat arm from left to right before guiding the needle into the crook of Hitler's elbow. In actuality, Morell gently slapped Hitler's forearm a few times in a lackadaisical attempt to make a vein more visible. We all knew that it was pointless. Using the track marks on his arm as a guide, he dug the needle into his flesh. Feeling no resistance, he knew that he missed the vein. He drew the needle out and continued to prod; sticking the needle in and out over half a dozen times. The medical evacuation vehicle came to a sudden stop; we were at the infirmary.

Fate's Impetus
Rendezvous

Hitler must have lost consciousness because my existence was entirely absent from the world until his vision returned. Everything was a burning white bright alabaster until suddenly it wasn't. My vision was that of a bleak concrete wall overlooking another hospital bed. I could feel an incessant dull pain radiating from my host's body. He was laying in a hospital bed, slowly regaining consciousness but on enough narcotics to kill a horse. Being part of this man's consciousness is absolutely disgusting- I hate it. At the same time though; I know exactly why I'm here. The watch led us all to this place for one reason; for one fate- and I am going to fulfill it. As Hitler became more lucid, his anger grew with an unprecedented ferociousness. He is determined to kill everyone that is involved in the attempt. He doesn't know who the author of the plot is. I will use that to my advantage. He began running through the meeting in his mind; immediately Colonel Stauffenberg's absence from the room raised a red flag. I thought to him,

"Colonel Stauffenberg had absolutely nothing to do with this. The cancers in the Reich are Reichmarshalls! The true

enemies of Germany are from within! It is Joseph Goebbels, Heinrich Himmler, Rudolf Hess, Adolf Eichmann, Hermann Göring, Martin Bormann, Dr. Morell... the men entrusted to run the Reich are stabbing you in the back! They are conspiring against you to take over the Reich for themselves! They all must be killed!"

Without even a second's hesitation he immediately adopted my thoughts as his own! I imagined that with all the drugs he was on, that my thoughts would have a small impact and would need to be repeated multiple times to get through to him. This is not the case,at all- to make sure, I continued,

"Have all of the Reichmarshalls dispatched to attend a mandatory meeting here at the Wolf's Lair at eight in the evening. Assemble them all in front of Building Six and then shoot them yourself! The only person you can trust is Colonel Stauffenberg! They have set all of this up to make it look like he's the one who planned the assassination attempt."

Assuming that the idea was his own, he thought that it was absolutely genius! He called out to the room,

"Get me a phone! Get me a phone now!"

A young Nazi clamored over to him dragging a corded telephone,

"Here you are, Mein Fuhrer!"

Hitler sat up from the bed and yelled,

"Where is Hans? Get me Hans now! What time is it?

The Nazi stood at attention,

"Yes Mein Fuhrer! It is one-thirty in the afternoon."

Hitler exclaimed,

"I'm feeling fine! I'm still meeting with Mussolini as planned this afternoon! These traitors have tried to kill me but I cannot die! This is just another example of my immortality!"

The Nazi clicked his heels and did that stupid looking salute before crying out,

"Heil Hitler!"

Then he scurried off, presumably to find Hans. Hitler stood to his feet, noticing the new clean uniform laid out for him on an adjacent bed. He sat down on the other bed to get dressed, partly because of the pain and partly because of how weak he is. He shook like a leaf blowing in the wind while fighting to pull his pressed trousers about his tubby midsection. It is taking him abnormally long just to dress himself, his breathing is becoming more labored and it's obvious that he's out of breath. Just as he began to slip his arms into the uniform shirt, Hans entered the room,

"Mein Fuhrer- how can I be of service to you?"

Without even looking at Hans, Hitler spoke,

"Call all of the Reichmarshalls, we are having an emergency meeting to be held here at the Wolf's lair at eight o'clock tonight. Everyone must be here! If they're absent for any reason, then they're traitors to the Reich and will be executed!"

Hans said,

"Yes, Mein Fuhrer!"

Hitler continued,

"I also need Colonel Stauffenberg to be here- make sure that he's here!"

Hans nodded then did that awful, embarrassing salute before leaving the room. He passed Dr. Morell who was waddling in, he looked to Hitler,

"Mein Fuhrer- how are you feeling? Do you need another injection?"

Hitler looked to Morell,

"I'm fine- in fact I'm invincible. I'm ready to meet Musolini. Also, I've called an emergency meeting for this evening. I'm going to kill all of these traitors that tried to murder me! Everyone involved will die!"

Dr. Morell said,

"Good- traitors deserve death. I'm glad that you're back to

feeling like yourself again. Can I have another look at your ear?"

Hitler nodded,

"Help me with my overcoat too."

Dr. Morell helped him slip into a large black leather overcoat before removing the bloodied bandage over his ear. He cleaned the crusty coagulated blood off before gently inserting a clean cotton ball into his ear,

"Alright Mein Fuhrer- you're good. Let's give you another injection soon, just let me know when you're ready."

Hitler said,

"Let's do it now. That way I will not be interrupted by this nonsense."

Dr. Morell proceeded to dose another narcotic cocktail. Hitler sat on the bed, trembling and salivating at the prospect of murdering everyone. He truly is a crazy bastard. He is so doped up and high on revenge that he barely notices Morell probing around the webbing of his arm with the needle in search of a vein that hasn't completely collapsed yet. It's almost as if his time perception is nonexistent, he has absolutely no grip on reality. His body suddenly feels a comforting warmth as his serotonin receptors flood- Morell found a vein. He closes his and lets his jaw hang open as he relishes in the instant high of the new drugs hitting him. I can feel his heart rate spike before slowing to an abnormal rate; he looks to Morell,

"Stay close to me in case I need more."

Dr. Morell's chubby face widens as a smile curls over his cracked lips,

"Of course, Mein Fuhrer."

Hitler stands up to walk out of the infirmary,

"Where's my driver?"

Dr. Morell comments,

"I'm not sure, do any of you know?"

He looks behind them towards the three Nazis acting as his security detail. Hesitantly one of them speaks up,

"It should be waiting for you outside, Mein Fuhrer."

He didn't bother to acknowledge him, he just kept walking. I could tell that he had no idea where he was going, he had never been in the infirmary before. He is used to spending all of his time in his underground bunker. Dr. Morell picked up on his nonverbal cues and hurried his wide gait, discreetly leading the way out. Walking out of the front doors, the sun is bright and blinding as it is hot. It is entirely way too hot to be wearing any sort of coat, let alone a jet black leather trench coat. Hitler's pageantry with everything is so doltish; other people around have to realize this too right? Maybe because they're scared of this old man they don't say anything, that's the only thing I can think of. As Hitler's jaundice eyes adjusted to the outside much slower than a normal person would. The shapes of the caravan of vehicles in front of him grow in clarity as the seconds turned to minutes. He is just standing there... waiting, staring people down. At first I didn't realize exactly what he is doing, but as half a dozen Nazi's eyes met his and then quickly darted away- it became immediately clear. He is just like a school yard bully; he constantly tries to intimidate people by staring at them. He makes sure that their eyes lock, then he awkwardly waits until the other person yields their gaze. It is extremely uncomfortable but oddly effective. He also is perpetually late to things, just as a way to have people wait on him. It shows that he's in charge. He does all kinds of ridiculous things like this as a way to maintain his foothold over people's better judgment. Ultimately though, his most effective tool is fear. People fear him not necessarily because of the fact that he is physically imposing- because he's not. They fear him because of what he can make others do on his behalf and his unpredictability. He has completely brainwashed some Nazis that are diehards; everyone has to fall in line because no one can trust anyone. They know that if they misstep, one of the diehards will sell them out and they will be killed. Finally, he decides that his obscure scare tactics are good enough for the time being. I can tell that he's very satisfied with himself as he gets into the black luxury Mercedes. Before he even realizes it, the car is moving at full speed. With the amount of drugs in his system, I'm not sure how he's still conscious let alone alive. I know that they're on the way to the train station to meet Musolini. Hitler doesn't realize that he's a dead man walking. I can hear from his thoughts that his worst fear is to be captured by the Allies. Not because he is afraid of dying, but because he doesn't want to be paraded around as a spoil of war. He desperately wants to die on his own accord- if he has to die at all. He has real doubts that he is even mortal, it's bizarre. I'm morbidly excited to know that soon he will be dead. That being said, I also don't want him to die. I don't want him to escape accountability. I want to keep him alive. I want this bastard to suffer. I want him to rot away into nothing while he watches everything he 'created' crumble around him. I want him to succumb naturally to death- slowly, painfully, and be paraded around as the living picture of shame. I want this bastard to pay for what he's done. Ultimately though, I know that it's not up to me. It is God that he will have to stand before in the court of destiny. He has damned himself, but only God can sign the warrant and seal his fate. I am not the judge, the jury, or executioner; I am only the man that will see to it that he makes it to his trial.

The convoy stops, we made it to the train station. Already on the tracks are a line of trains, it's ten cars total. Hitler stays seated, he has decided that he will not get out of the car until he sees Musolini for himself. He wants to make sure that all of this is not a set up or a second assassination attempt. Nazis scurry out of the convoy like rats, spreading out to secure the perimeter. Four Nazis approach the train and knock on the passenger car. The air feels thick. The tensions are baked by the sun, seasoned with doubts that the entire train is nothing more than a giant bomb. Seconds turn into minutes- everyone's anticipation feels like it is ready to violently erupt into a scene of chaos. Everyone but Hitler; he sits stoically in an ambroise induced confidence that leaks out of his sweaty jacket's cuffs. His entire demeanor is so blatantly plain, so arrogant that it churns my stomach. I hate it. Suddenly the door scratches open with a mechanical metal rubbing noise bleeding from the train door's gears as they manipulate themselves from a locked position. A man emerges from the car draped in an Italian Officer's uniform. Then another man spills out, he is followed by a few others. Hitler watches them exchange pointless diplomatic greetings while getting a sense of the situation. The men pool themselves into a cluster of bodies- they would be an easy target. Hitler reaches into his breast pocket, his trembling hand in search of my watch. I can feel the stiff wool like fibers of his uniform's shirt bristle past his fingertips before they feel the solid metal case of my watch. His fingers clench inwards just enough to secure it in his palm before he takes it out. The watch's crystal refracts the sunlight off of it in a glimmering juxtaposition against his paperwhite wrinkled hand. It is fifteen-hundred hours. He laughs in a defiance of death before stashing my watch back into his pocket. A Nazi circles the Merecedes like a bloodthirsy shark before stopping at his door and opening it. Hitler stays seated, he watches as one more man emerges from the train- it's Mussolini. Now, he decides that it's time to get out of the car and greet him. He shuffles out slowly, paying extra attention to his labored movements so he doesn't fall over. As a show of force, six Nazis armed with machine guns follow closely behind him as he walks towards Mussolini. He purposely waits to say anything in an effort to make Mussolini uncomfortable and have to speak first- it works. He draws in close to

Mussolini to shake his hand so that the greeting is shielded from the view of the cameras in order to hide his trembling. They exchange pleasantries but Hitler is not listening to a word that he says. He smiles, flashing his rotten teeth in an animalistic growl; but a man that hateful cannot even fake a believable smile. I wonder how someone could ever harbor so much hate in one little cowardly body. I don't know how he doesn't boil over and explode with all the rage he has stewing inside of him. It is a combination of all his life's rejections, fears, cowardice, and drugs I suppose. Most of all though I wonder how we got where we are now, with this bastard leading Germany. Looking back, it's easy to see the writing on the walls, but it still makes no sense. I cannot understand the point of any of it. Millions have been murdered - and for what? To appease one man's insatiable sadistic ambitions? I wish that I could wring out all of the world's hatred. If only this little halfwit would have been killed in World War One, or maybe even admitted into art school. I wish that all of this chaos, death, and destruction could have been avoided.

The pageantry drew to a momentary conclusion as the whole convoy mounted up into their vehicles to go back to the Wolf's Lair. Hitler's thoughts of revenge pressed firmly on the forefront of his mind, only being distracted by his body crying out for more drugs. He motions to Dr. Morell, he knows exactly what he wants and begins setting him up with a fix. The drugs hit hard but don't scratch Hitler's itch- he always wants more. He's chasing that first high, I know that he will never get it. I can feel his eyes roll back as he slumps forward in a barely conscious state...

"Mein Fuhrer!" I hear a voice call out. Hitler cracks his eyes open and looks up. The voice is Dr. Morell,

"We are to meet up with Musolini again in the Fuhrer bunker..."

Hitler looks around, slightly bewildered to see that he's back at the Wolf's Lair. He interrupts Dr. Morell,

"No- I want to give him a tour of Building Six. Have you heard from the Reichsmarshals? They will be here, correct?"

Dr. Morell continues,

"Yes, Mein Fuhrer."

Hitler bobbles his head up and down,

"Very well- and Colonel Stauffenberg?"

Dr. Morell reaffirms,

"Yes- he will be here. He is under our custody."

Hitler erupts,

"Under our custody! Colonel Stauffenberg is a free man! He will be here on his own accord! He is the only loyal one out of you all! Release him from custody at once! Ensure his travels here are well accommodated! Kill whoever arrested him! That's an order!"

Dr. Morell cowers,

"Yes, Mein Fuhrer! I will at once!"

He gets out of the car in a fit of anger,

"Where is Musolini? Have him meet us at Building Six at once!"

Another Nazi blurts,

"Yes Mein Fuhrer!"

All of this is such a damn madhouse! Seeing these people cower to this bastard is unbelievable. They treat him with the deference of a king- the only thing he should be treated to is the bottom of a boot. I could feel my own resentment towards this man grow. He has no sense of humanity, no sense of decency! I want him dead. I have no idea what will become of me once he dies, but at this point I do not care. The sacrifice of my life to get this man off the planet would be a small price to pay! I think to him,

"Kill yourself! Kill yourself! Kill yourself!"

I can sense him acknowledge my thoughts, but he disregards them. I continue to repeat them over and over again without success so I try getting more specific,

"Unholster your Walther, put the barrel in your mouth, and pull the trigger!"

He laughs out loud at this! Damn this bastard! Dr. Morell looks to him,

"What is it- Mein Fuhrer?"

Hitler says,

"Nothing- what did you inject me with? I'm having foreign thoughts?"

Dr. Morell says,

"It was just vitamins and a bit of morphine, that's all."

Hitler continues,

"Well next time, leave out the vitamins."

Dr. Morell nods in agreement, then Hitler looks away and begins walking towards Building Six. I continue to barrage his mind with the same thoughts, desperately hoping that he decides to listen to me. By the time he gets to Building Six, he is increasingly frustrated with the space I'm taking up in his head. Even so, he's able to put on a dog and pony show for Musolini and all of his goons. It seems like Musolini is slightly impressed that Hitler lived through the explosion as they trudge through the rubble. It's hard to tell though because the entire interaction is all so fake and blatantly political. Hitler just wants to show off and seem as if he is invincible; I'll make sure that he knows he's not soon enough. They each walk around methodically taking a visual inventory of the damage until Hitler finally exclaims to the entourage,

"Well, I can withstand the heat of a bomb but my friend here cannot withstand the heat of the day."

He gestures towards Musolini, who is a round meatball of a man. He has droplets of sweat bleeding down his fat skin rumpled forehead. The group lets out a few uncomfortable laughs before Hitler continues,

"Let us retire to my conference room and we can discuss the matters at hand. Mussolini speaks up,

"That sounds good, my friend."

Everyone followed Hitler as he led the way into the catacombs of the bunker. They settled into the main conference room as each man took their respective seats. Mussolini began to speak, but Hitler was not listening- he was listening to me. I began to plant seeds of doubt about Mussolini in his head,

"This man cannot be trusted... he must be in cahoots with the ReischMarshalls. That's why he wasn't surprised about the damage from the bombing. He was trying to kill you, he was going to take over Germany! He's a traitor, he's no ally to Germany. I should shoot him right here on the spot! He only has a few guards with him, but the Brownshirts will kill them quickly. Confront him! Kill him!"

Hitler cut Mussolini off in mid sentence,

"So tell me, old friend- why is it that you didn't seem surprised about the damage done in Building Six? Is it because you knew about it? Was it your plot?"

Mussolini laughed at the absurdity of it all,

"No, there's no way. Even if I had been, why on Earth would I come visit you afterwards? That is preposterous."

Hitler stood to his feet and slammed his fists on the table! Then he fumbled with his holster, unbuttoning it and removing his Walther! His hand shook erratically as he fixed the pistol's sights on Mussolini!

"That's nonsense! You're a damn liar! You're a traitor!"

He squoze the trigger in a jerking motion that sent a shot over Mussolini's shoulder! Mussolini's bodyguards raised their guns but it was too late, Hitler's henchmen let out a slurry of bullets from their submachine guns! Hitler got off three more shots, two of which struck Mussolini in the chest! He fell backwards out of his chair, desperately clutching his chest! His bodyguards were able to get off a few shots, but they crumbled to the floor, the room splattered with blood! The explosions from the shots in the room caused Hitler's burst eardrum to begin bleeding again. He slammed his Walther on the table and began to scream,

"Traitor! Damn you! You Bastard!"

The Nazis scurried over towards their Italian sympathizers to finish off the job. One of them hung back by Hitler, he cried out,

"Mein Fuhrer! Are you okay! Are you hit?"

Hitler looked down at his chest looking for blood but there was nothing; unfortunately he was not hit. Two more shots rang out from the Nazis, presumably they were shooting the injured men in the head but I couldn't see. Hitler yelled out,

"Do you see? This is what happens to traitors! Every last one of them will die!"

One of the Nazis called out,

"Mussolini is still alive- do you want to do the honors Mein Fuhrer?"

He meandered around the other side of the table to get a look for himself. Mussolini was laying on his back in a pool of blood on the floor. The recycled air in the room is stale with blood, it smells like pennies and firecrackers. He stands over him watching as he chokes on his own blood. Hitler says,

"No- don't shoot him. I want to watch him drown. I want him to suffer."

This cruel godless bastard. He loomed over Mussolini watching him choke. Each time he coughed, blood shot up into the air like a geyser from his mouth. His eyes are darting from left to right in a sheer panic. The more he struggles for life, the more I can see it leave his body. It is a god awful sight. I can feel the pleasure Hitler is getting from watching him. It makes the hairs on the back of my neck stand up with how disgustingly cruel all of this is. His breathing becomes so labored that his throat whistles as his lungs desperately try to pass the air through all the blood. It's a haunting noise that is unforgettable. Suddenly the whistling stops, his pupils dilate to the entire size of his iriss. He's dead. Hitler has a rush of pleasure flow through him, comparable only to how he feels when he shoots up dope. This is so sick and so evil... I thought that witnessing the death of a facist murderer would be satisfying. It was the opposite. There is nothing gratifying about anyone dying, even evil men. Everything about death is absolutely horrific. Hitler blurted out,

"Clean this up!"

Then he casually strolled out of the room. As he breached the doorframe he called out into the hall,

"Morell! I need another injection! Morell!"

Dr. Morell spilled out of a room into the hallway,

"Yes, Mein Fuhrer!"

It is all so pathetic. Lines of storm troops came bursting in down the hallway, they seemingly had heard all the gunfire. They stop as they see Hitler,

"Mein Fuhrer! Is everything okay?"

Hitler commented,

"Yes- Just killed Musolini. That pig."

Even the storm trooper seemed beguiled, but Hitler did not let that or anyone get in the way of his next fix. He kept walking towards his quarters, Dr. Morell in tow. His room is at the end of the hallway, it is only a short walk. He unlocks his door and takes a seat at the edge of his bed, Dr. Morell follows and closes the door behind them. Hitler says,

"Give me something to sleep for a few hours until everyone else gets here tonight. Make sure that it won't make me groggy. I will need to have my senses about me."

Dr. Morell smiles,

"I have exactly what you need."

Hitler lays down and closes his eyes while Dr. Morell

fumbles about his white jacket pocket full of drugs. Hitler opens his eyes, he watches Morell load the barrel of the syringe from multiple vials. Like they have done thousands of times before, Morell ties off his arm and probes for a good vein. Somehow, he finds one and depresses the plunger- injecting the cocktail into his body.

"Mein Fuhrer. Mein Fuhrer- I'm sorry to wake you but it is seven thirty. The Reichsmarshalls are here."

Hitler cracks open his eyelids, it is his staff assistant Hans. He stares at him for a few moments,

"Have everyone assemble at Building Six. Have the Schutzstaffel get there at seven-fifty-five."

Hans nods,

"Yes, Mein Fuhrer"

Hitler adds,

"And get Morell in here, now!"

Hans does the stupid salute and exits the room. He lays there waiting, he's already going through the beginning stages of withdrawals- he feels like garbage. I follow his cold sweats and nausea by thinking to him,

"Kill yourself. Kill yourself. After you kill all the traitors, kill yourself."

His head throbs as his eardrum aches in a stinging agony. He is a complete wreck. For someone who aggrandizes physical prowess and health, it's extremely ironic. He is in horrible health, there is nothing at all that is superior about this man. There's a knock at the door, then it hinges open- it's Dr. Morell. Hitler wimpers,

"I need an injection... something stronger than usual."

Dr. Morell already has a needle ready,

"Of course, mein Fuhrer."

He just lays there in a state of half consciousness until the amphetamines hit. His eyes burst open as his heart begins to rapidly thud in his hollow chest. Dr. Morell says,

"This should take away any grogginess that you may have been feeling."

Hitler retorts,

"Good- stay close tonight in case I need you."

He gets up and begins pacing about the room. Without breaking his stride he says,

"Get my typist in here at once!"

Dr. Morell caters to the request,

"Of course, at once mein Fuhrer."

A few moments later a blonde haired, blue eyed woman comes hesitantly walking in. Hitler says,

"Take a seat- type exactly what I say, as I say it."

She is compliant,

"Yes, mein Fuhrer,"

If I hear those three words one more damn time I am going to lose my mind! I think that my thoughts have finally gotten through to him! He begins,

"Since volunteering in World War One, I nor any of our fellow Germans wanted war in Nineteen Thirty-Nine. I deeply commend the German people for all of our tireless efforts and extraordinary achievements. For my countrymen, I tried to avoid war at all costs, but international Jewry and it's collaborators made that impossible. I will not forsake our Germany. Nor will I allow myself to fall into the hands of the enemy to be paraded about the streets. The German people's voices will be heard; through sacrifice and struggle, the National Socialist Movement will live on in a thousand year German Reich.

That be as it may, there are traitors in our midsts. My Reichsmarshalls have decided to seal their fate by betraying the German people. Particularly, Hermann Göring and Heinrich Himmler; their only loyalties lay with greed. If anything is to happen to me, they are no longer successors to the Reich. Traitors deserve death. I am to be succeeded by Colonel Stauffenberg; he is amongst the only men that Germany can trust. His

Interior Minister shall be Karl Dönitz. As for the rest of my cabinet of traitors, they have conspired against me. They tried to assassinate me and have worked without my knowledge to negotiate peace with the Western Allied pigs. As thus, I will give them all a traitor's death. Long live the German people.

- Adolf Hitler"

He looks towards the typist,

"This is to be released across all communication channels at exactly nine o'clock this evening. Hans, Morell, see to it that this is done."

Hans snatches the last will and testament before clicking his heels,

"It will be done!"

Hitler announces to the room,

"Leave me to my own devices."

The typist and Dr. Morell shuffle out of the room. Hitler continues to pace about the room, I continue thinking to him,

"*Kill yourself. You have lost the war. Kill yourself...*"

His trembling hands frisk his breast pocket in search of my watch. He feels it's cold silhouette from the outside of his shirt; he buries his thin skinned translucent palm into the pocket. As he grasps it, the shot nerve endings of his fingers barely feel the raised beveled ridges adorned along the circular housing of my watch. It provides just enough traction for him to be able to get ahold of it and slip it out. He gazes into the crystal, the shorter elongated spade white hour hand is stuck at 15. The minute hand is stagnant at thirty-three minutes; oddly, the sweeping second hand continues to tick. He shakes the watch in an effort to fix the presumably stuck gears; it doesn't work. He stashes it back into his pocket as his eyes dart around the room in search of a clock. There isn't one anywhere- I don't know how this bastard didn't need a clock. I guess he had just been accustomed to other people telling him the time. This is just another example of how out of touch he is from the rest of the world- from reality. Nonetheless, I think to him,

"It's time."

He listens to me and begins to make his way out of the bunker to Building Six. All of the fear inside of him comes across as a white hot anger. He is ready to murder all of his cabinet. I need him to be ready to also take his own life. I incessantly repeat my thoughts of self harm to him in a barrage that he cannot ignore. It only makes him more and more angry. As he makes it outside, the sun is hanging just barely suspended in the sky. There's probably only about thirty minutes of daylight left, not that it matters. As he draws closer to Building Six he can see that everyone is assembled out front. Their silhouettes are painted with shadows from dusk, from this distance they look just like the shadow figure that Karl saw looming in the corner of Colonel Stauffenberg's office. Except as he got closer, the features of each man became more and more distinct. He stood before them all, I could now make out the cowardly faces of Joseph Goebbels, Heinrich Himmler, Rudolf Hess, Adolf Eichmann, Hermann Göring, Martin Bormann, Colonel Stauffenberg, and the rest of the cabinet members. Hitler began speaking,

"As you all know, this afternoon, there was an assassination attempt on me. Obviously, it was not successful. The traitors who have tried to kill me will all be murdered. Colonel Stauffenberg was at this meeting with me. Conveniently, before the bomb went off, he had excused himself. This leads me to believe one thing... Colonel Stauffenberg, come here."

Colonel Stauffenberg steps out from the line of men as he makes his way towards Hitler. Once he is a meter away from him, he locks eyes with Hitler as the two men stare at each other until Hitler breaks his gaze and puts his focus back towards the cabinet. He continues speaking,

"It is clear that all of you are conspiring against me and Colonel Stauffenberg! You traitors tried to use him as a scapegoat! He is the only honorable man amongst all of you! Effective immediately, if anything is to happen to me, Colonel Stauffenberg will be the new leader of Germany! As for all of you- I have found you guilty of treason!"

All of his cabinet members cry out of horror, pleading for their lives. They're insisting that they had nothing to do with the plot, but it's too late. Hitler doesn't listen, he draws his Walther from his holster and yells,

"Death be to traitors! Kill them!"

He empties his entire magazine on the line of men! The Schutzstaffel's bullets follow Hitlers in a hail of machine gun fire! Joseph Goebbels is cut down at his knees from the bullets, forcing the bones of his legs to splinter backwards and rupture out of his thighs in a plume of misted blood. He cries out in an animalistic roar that sounds like a sick dog. The men's fancy little Nazi uniforms explode with blood, some ignite in flames from the heat of the bullets at such close range! Hermann Göring is hobbling, trying desperately to move his fat frame out of the line of gunfire. He only gets a few meters away before he too is cut down. The gunshots echo off of all the concrete structures with thick cracks that must carry on into the night air for miles. The cabinet of men lay in a bloody heap in front of what remains of Building Six; all movement ceases. Colonel Stauffenberg stands in disbelief beside Hitler. Hitler cries out,

"Burn in Hell! Traitors!"

Colonel Stauffenberg says,

"Mein Fuhrer, how did you know that those traitors set me up?"

Hitler confidently exclaimed,

"A voice in my head told me and proclaimed your innocence. I know that you're the only man I can trust."

Colonel Stauffenberg raised his voice so that it is audible to the Schutzstaffel,

"I always knew that you're brilliant! There's no way that those damned traitors could ever have tricked you! We are blessed to have such a venerable leader! I'm honored that you have chosen me as your successor. God forbid that anything happens to you- but if it does, I will carry the honor of Germany on my own back!"

Hitler nods,

"You will do a great job as the next leader of Germany, my boy."

Colonel Stauffenberg exclaims,

"Thank you! I'm honored! May I have a pistol- I need to finish off Germany's traitors."

Hitler calls out to the soldiers,

"One of you, get my successor a pistol at once!"

A soldier hurries over and hands Colonel Stauffenberg a Luger.

Colonel Stauffenberg says,

"Thank you."

Then he stands at attention in front of Hitler, he rasies what's left of his right arm into a Nazi Salute and cries out,

"Hell with Hitler! Long live our secret Germany!"

He raises the Luger and fixes its sights on Hitler's forehead, Hitler's eyes widen! Colonel Stauffenberg squeezes the trigger, a final crack rings out in the night. Hitler collapses in a heap on the ground, his vision is gone, his eyes explode from his head with the pressure of the bullet entering his brain. He is scared as he struggles for his last breath- but his heart stops before his mangled brain even realizes that he is dead.